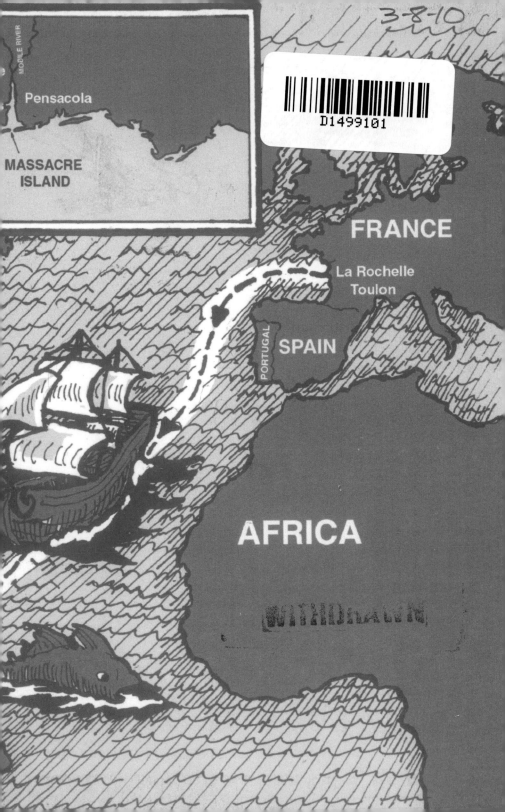

3-8-10

D1499101

Pensacola

MOBILE RIVER

MASSACRE
ISLAND

FRANCE

La Rochelle
Toulon

PORTUGAL

SPAIN

AFRICA

WITHDRAWN

Massacre

Island

WITHDRAWN

MASSACRE

ISLAND

Anne Chancey Dalton

Illustrated by Dave Edwards

Ann Chancey Dalton

BSB

BLACK SWANS BOOKS
Mobile, Alabama

WITHDRAWN

PROPERTY OF BCC
WALTON COUNTY PUBLIC
LIBRARY SYSTEM

Text copyright © 2002 by Anne Chancey Dalton
Illustrations copyright © 2002 by David C. Edwards

All rights reserved. No part of this publication may be reproduced or transmitted in any form or by any means, electronic or mechanical, including photocopy, recording, or any information storage and retrieval system without permission in writing from the publisher.

Requests for permission to make copies of any part of the work should be mailed to: Permissions Department, Black Swans Books, P. O. Box 1111, Mobile, AL 36623-1111.

Printed and bound in the United States of America.

Black Swans Books World Wide Web address:
www.blackswansbooks.com

Pre-press by:
Design Press, Inc.
Sycamore, FL

Publisher's Cataloging-in-Publication
(Provided by Quality Books, Inc.)

Dalton, Anne Chancey.
    Massacre Island / Anne Chancey Dalton ; illustrated by Dave Edwards. -- 1st ed.
    p. cm.
    Includes bibliographical references.
    SUMMARY: Historically accurate tale about French lands in the American south in the early 1700s.
    ISBN 0-9709534-0-2

    1. Mobile (Ala.)--History--Juvenile fiction.
    [1. Mobile (Ala.)--History--Fiction.] I. Edwards, Dave (David C.) II. Title.

PZ7.D1693Ma 2002   [Fic]
                    QBI98-500036

To Perry . . .
with love and gratitude
for always supporting
my many endeavors.

Acknowledgments

Many individuals invested time and energy to make this book possible. The inspiration for it came as a result of my involvement with Project Archaeology. Sponsored in the state by the Alabama Historical Commission in conjunction with the Bureau of Land Management, the project trains archaeologists, educators, and Native Americans to work as a team to help teachers incorporate archaeology into their lesson plans. Workshops are held at the University of South Alabama Center for Archaeological Studies through the South Alabama Research and Inservice Center. Ashley Dumas (presently at Moundville Archaeological Park), Debi Lawrence, and I presented the first workshop in 1996. Bonnie Gums is now the Project Archaeology coordinator, but all the archaeologists at USA help make the program a success. Most of them read the manuscript and made helpful suggestions. Ashley Dumas introduced me to archaeology at Old Mobile and told of her experiences on the dig at Dauphin Island, and the book evolved from there.

I am particularly grateful to Dr. Gregory Waselkov and Bonnie Gums, who not only read the manuscript but also answered innumerable questions and provided resource materials. George Shorter, who has done extensive research on Dauphin Island and led the archaeological excavation there, explained artifacts in the lab and was especially helpful on a tour of the island—pointing out the site of the original village.

I want to express thanks to others who read the manuscript for historical accuracy: Jay Higginbotham, Director of the Mobile Municipal Archives; John O'Donnell-Rosales, genealogical researcher specializing in military records; and Douglas Dillard, President of the Fort Toulouse Re-enactors.

I greatly appreciate teacher and Native American, Johnny Weaver. He gave insightful recommendations and worked on the Choctaw glossary with Luke Rivers and Peter Rivers, MOWA Choctaw genealogist. Dusty Collins also gave helpful comments on the glossary. Darla Graves, past executive director of Alabama Indian Affairs Commission, read the manuscript from a Native American perspective.

Evelyne Carro, Ann Miller, and Betsy Stokes gave invaluable assistance with the French vocabulary and glossary.

The re-enactors at Fort Toulouse generously answered questions and offered encouragement. I want to particularly thank Ned Jenkins, Lee Humphreys for information on food, and Doug Dillard for his enthusiastic support of the book.

Thanks to Leah Rawls Atkins who gave input on using "Life in La Louisiane" as a teaching tool. Carol Mader made beneficial suggestions after using the manuscript with her creative writing class.

Two fantastic editors, Carolyn Yoder and Betsy Stokes, made this endeavor a tremendous learning experience. Thanks a million times over to both of you!

I am grateful to Adele Head and the reference librarians at the Panama City Public Library for diligently searching out minute details for me.

A heartfelt thanks to friends who literally prayed me through this experience. It is not the same book as it would have been without those prayers!

Two friends tremendously influenced Massacre Island: Cheryl Foster and Susan Lewis laughed with me through these pages, when many times I would have given up in despair. You are both rare treasures!

To my unique family—which seems to grow daily— words cannot express my appreciation for your love, encouragement, and most of all, for giving me the freedom to be me. Life in our family is fun, and Thanksgiving is always around the corner.

CONTENTS

NOTE TO READERS

Mobile was the first French town in what is now the United States that still exists today—just as Plymouth was the first British and St. Augustine the first Spanish.

In 1697, King Louis XIV of France chose Pierre Le Moyne d'Iberville to establish a colony on the northern coast of the Gulf of Mexico. Iberville made two voyages to explore the area. He decided to build Fort Louis de La Louisiane on the Mobile River in present-day Alabama. The settlement near the fort was named La Mobile in honor of the Mobilian Indians.

In the fall of 1701, Governor Iberville, as he was called, sailed from France with soldiers, sailors, and colonists—all men, except four women and five children. He was seriously ill from an abscess in his side when the French ships anchored in Pensacola Bay in December. Unable to leave the Spanish port until he recovered, Iberville put his younger brother, Bienville, in charge of work on the fort and settlement.

Jean-Baptiste de Bienville had come to La Louisiane (French Louisiana) on Iberville's first voyage to the area. He became deputy commandant of Fort Maurepas in present-day Mississippi in 1701. After receiving orders from Iberville, Bienville began moving men and supplies from Fort Maurepas to Port Dauphin on Massacre Island. Since the Mobile River was too shallow for ships, a warehouse was built on the island to store supplies. These would be carried to the colony on small boats.

Monsieur Nicolas de La Salle was in charge of supplies, so he and his family sailed from Pensacola for Massacre Island on January 3, 1702, with workers, sailors and soldiers. The other women and children, some soldiers, and sailors stayed with Iberville on the ships in Pensacola Bay until time to move to La Mobile.

The characters in *Massacre Island* are people who really lived at that time—with two exceptions: Claude is based on cabin boys who sailed with Governor Iberville. Red Bird and his family are created from information on the Mobilian and Choctaw tribes of Native Americans. Most of the events in the book actually happened. The facts come from the journals of a ship's carpenter, a priest, a military officer, and Governor Iberville. "Life in La Louisiane" gives additional information about this period in history. To learn more about what was happening before the story began, turn to page 166.

Iberville and Bienville
French Settlement of the Gulf Coast

1699

Jan.	Iberville and Bienville arrive on the Gulf Coast
Feb.	Exploration of Massacre Island and present-day Mississippi
Mar.	Exploration of present-day Louisiana and Mississippi River
Apr.	Fort Maurepas (Fort Biloxi) built (present-day Ocean Springs, MS)
May	Iberville leaves for France
Sept.	Iberville sails from France for La Louisiane
Dec.	Iberville arrives at Fort Maurepas

1700

Feb.	Fort Boulaye (Fort MS) built (present-day Myrtle Grove, LA) Bienville (age 20) becomes commandant of Fort Boulaye
May	Iberville leaves for France

1701

Sept	Iberville leaves France with colonists Bienville (age 21) becomes commandant of Fort Maurepas
Dec.	Iberville and colonists arrive at Santa María de Galve (present-day Pensacola, FL)

1702

Jan. 3	La Salle family and others sail from Pensacola to Massacre Island
Jan. 11	Bienville and others travel up Mobile River to select La Mobile site
Jan. 20	Land at Twenty-seven Mile Bluff dedicated for La Mobile and Fort Louis
Feb.15	Iberville leaves Pensacola for Massacre Island and La Mobile
Mar.11	La Salle family moves from Massacre Island to La Mobile
Mar.	Bienville (age 22) becomes commandant of Fort Louis
Apr. 27	Iberville leaves Pensacola for France

The French Gulf Coast
1660–1770

1660—

1661—— Pierre Le Moyne (Iberville) born in Montreal, Canada

1680—— Jean-Baptiste Le Moyne (Bienville) born in Montreal, Canada

1682—— Robert Cavelier de La Salle explores Mississippi River to the Gulf of Mexico

1684—— Robert Cavelier de La Salle tries to set up a French colony in present-day Texas

1698–99——Iberville's First Voyage to La Louisiane—leaves France in Nov. 1698

1699–00——Iberville's Second Voyage—leaves France in Sept. 1699

1701–02——Iberville's Third Voyage—leaves France in Sept. 1701

1704——Cassette Girls arrive in La Mobile

1706——Iberville dies in Havana, Cuba

1711——La Mobile moved to Mobile's present location

1714——Fort Jean Baptiste built (present-day Natchitoches, LA)

1716——Fort Rosalie built (present-day Natchez, MS)

1717——Fort Toulouse built (present-day Wetumpka, AL)

1718——Bienville founds New Orleans

1718–22——New Biloxi (present day Biloxi, MS) becomes capital of La Louisiane

1720——Fort Louis's name changed to Fort Condé

1762——After French and Indian War, present-day Louisiana becomes Spanish

1763——Present-day western Florida, Alabama and Mississippi become British

1767——Bienville (age 87) dies in Paris, France

1770—

NARROW ESCAPE

January 5, 1702

Nicolas La Salle watched fear creep across his little brother's face.

Simon shivered and asked, "Who chopped off their heads?"

Nicolas pulled his blue coat tighter to keep out the cold ocean spray as they stood on the deck of the small ship, *Dauphine,* sailing from Pensacola to Mobile Bay. He knew his story froze Simon's insides, so Nicolas tried to sound brave as he said, "Probably pirates." But every night he dreaded going to sleep, because he had nightmares about the island.

"Tell me again what you heard," said eight-year-old Simon.

Nicolas took a deep breath. "Soon after we sailed from France on the *Renommée,* I heard Governor Iberville talking to Papa. The governor said he named it Massacre Island, because he and his men found a pile of skulls and bones. It hadn't been too many years since the massacre, because the people's belongings hadn't rotted."

Simon let out a sob and threw his arms around Nicolas's waist. "I don't want my head chopped off."

Moments later, when Nicolas saw his mother come out on deck, he gently pushed Simon away. "Here comes Maman. We've got to go."

Madame La Salle pulled the hood of her green wool cloak over her bonnet and tied it securely. Even though she was average height, she looked small as she inched across the slippery deck in the early morning light. However, her look of determination made up for her slender build. She called, "Nicolas and Simon, your father wants you to come below. You'll catch your death out here in this cold wind." She looked from Simon's tear-streaked face to Nicolas. "What's wrong?"

Nicolas yelled over the howling wind, "He's afraid to stay on the island."

"Have you scared him with foolish tales?" When Nicolas shrugged, his mother waved her hand at Simon as if to say forget about it. But Nicolas saw her frightened look when Papa told her how the island got its name. Now she motioned for them to follow as she headed toward the ship's hatch.

The cabin smelled stale from so many crowded in the small space for over two days. Men either milled around talking or lay in their bunks. The boys followed their mother to the small area where they spent most of their time. Five-year-old François was asleep in a bunk. Monsieur Nicolas La Salle sat with his broad shoulders hunched over a ledger lying open on a barrel he used as a desk. He was checking the supply list for La Mobile, the new settlement to be built up the Mobile River.

"Nicolas frightened Simon with silly stories," said their mother.

Their father pushed back the long dark curls of his wig, took off his glasses, and rubbed his eyes. He finally said to Nicolas. "I told you one tribe probably attacked another. It doesn't have anything to do with us, so don't worry about it."

Nicolas said, "I wanted Simon to know . . . in case we come across skeletons while we're hunting or exploring the island."

"The only place Iberville found bones was at the southwest end." He gave Nicolas a stern look. "You stay away from there."

"*Oui,** Papa." That was three years ago, thought Nicolas. No telling what's happened since then. Skeletons might be all over the place. One tribe may have attacked another, but I wish I could find out exactly what really happened and why.

"There won't be time for exploring anyway," said his father. "A large twelve-year-old like you will be too busy working."

Several people were gathering around a priest at the other end of the cabin. Monsieur La Salle stood. "Ah, I'd forgotten Père Dongé is saying Mass before the ship gets into the harbor." He looked at François still sleeping soundly. "Just let him sleep, Madelaine. We can see him if he wakes."

*See the glossaries for definitions and pronunciations of foreign words.

As Père Dongé finished Mass, a sailor came down the steep steps from the main deck and announced, "The winds are too strong for the ship to enter Pelican Island harbor. We're going to drop anchor outside the inlet and unload the cargo onto boats."

Monsieur La Salle frowned and said to his wife, "I don't want to lose supplies in these rough seas." Grabbing his hat, he said, "I'm going up on deck to see what's happening. You get our belongings together and have Nicolas and Simon bring them up when I send for them." He turned and followed the sailor.

Nicolas and Simon scrambled around, putting things into the trunk and tying up bundles, while their mother dressed François in warm clothes. After two days of being jammed in the cabin, Nicolas was glad they'd soon be on land. Since he was busy, he didn't have to think about the mournful sound of the wind and the anxious shouts on deck. It wasn't long before a sailor came for the trunk and told the boys their father wanted them. They put on their heavy *capotes,* the coats their mother had made for them from blue blankets before they left France.

As the boys scurried toward the door, she called, "Wait!" As she handed each son a *toque,* she said, "I didn't make these for nothing." Simon and Nicolas pulled on the red woolen stocking caps.

Madame La Salle said, "Nicolas, give that bundle to your father and then come back and get François. I can't get up those steps with him and our basket of food."

"But Maman! Papa said . . . ."

"Tell him I must have your help!"

Nicolas grumbled to himself all the way topside. When he came out on the deck, the freezing wind cut through his *capote*. He pulled the coat's hood over his *toque* and folded the sleeves over his hands. The heavy clouds made the sky dark and dreary, even though it was well past daybreak. Nicolas handed the bundle to his father and told him about François.

Monsieur La Salle slung the bundle against the side of the ship. "Get him up here within the minute!"

Nicolas dashed down to get his brother. He fidgeted while his mother slowly made her way up the steps with the basket. François, grouchy from being awakened, and scared by the sailors' shouts and the roar of the wind, refused to go up the steps. Nicolas practically dragged him topside. The chubby little boy squirmed and yelled, trying to get loose from Nicolas. However, it only took one look from his father, and he straightened up.

Monsieur La Salle herded his family toward the side of the ship. A large open boat bobbed like a toy on the rolling sea.

Madame La Salle turned pale at the sight of the boat below. A rope ladder flapped against the side of the *Dauphine.* She gave her husband a desperate look. "Oh my! I'll never be able to get down there."

"You must go immediately! The wind is getting stronger." Monsieur La Salle's expression softened slightly as he said, "The sailors are capable men and know how to handle the boat in this weather. Keep the boys seated and holding tight. You'll soon be on land."

Blinking back tears, Simon asked, "Aren't you coming, Papa?"

"No, I've got to see to the supplies."

Nicolas said, "If the supplies wash overboard, we'll starve this winter."

"We wouldn't starve," said his father, "but I know from experience we'd have a difficult time."

Père Dongé stepped forward. "Madame, we have a similar problem." He gestured at the black ankle-length garment of a priest showing under his dark woolen cloak. "I'll go down first, and maybe you can learn from my mistakes." He took off his wide-brimmed hat, folded it, and stuck it in a large leather bag. He put the strap of the bag over his head and across his chest to free his hands. Then he gave her an encouraging smile, made his way over the side of the ship, and slowly moved down the ladder. About halfway, he looked up and called, "I'll be waiting to help if you need me."

Madame La Salle's eyes had not left him. She smiled slightly and nodded. Then she gave her husband a tight hug and said, "Be careful!" With her jaw set, she followed Père Dongé.

The wind stung Nicolas's eyes as he watched a three-mast open boat draw near the *Dauphine*. Captain Joseph Le Moyne and his brother, Antoine, were in it. The sight of the captain brought back memories of a terrifying night several months earlier. He was captain of the

6

Palmier, the other ship sailing with the *Renommée* and two smaller vessels. North of Hispaniola, pirates had attacked the ships during a storm. From the deck of the *Renommée,* Nicolas had seen lightning strike the mainmast of the *Palmier* and split it in two. He had felt as if he'd been struck himself. He knew pirates overran ships and killed people. By some miracle the ships escaped. But now storms reminded him of pirates.

He glanced at the boat below. When his mother and Père Dongé were seated, two strong sailors carried François and Simon down on their backs. François whimpered until he was sitting between his mother and Père Dongé, but Simon looked too scared to make a sound. When the sailor put him down in the boat, Simon's legs buckled, and he fell to the floor. The sailor lifted him like a rag doll and sat him beside his mother.

Monsieur La Salle put his arm around Nicolas's shoulder and said, *"Mon fils,* my son, I'm counting on you to take care of your mother and brothers."

Nicolas looked deep into his father's eyes. Finally in a weak voice, he said, *"Oui,* Papa." He carefully climbed over the side of the ship. His heart fluttered as he moved one foot and then the next down the rope ladder. The water made his eyes burn, and he constantly licked his salty lips. A strong gust of wind almost blew him into the water even though he clutched the rungs so tightly they cut into his hands. When his feet touched the solid floor of the boat, he dropped into the seat in front of his mother and brothers. He tried to calm his racing heart

by watching a sailor lower a net containing the bundles and basket into the boat.

As the boat tossed to and fro, the crew pulled the oars with all their strength. Waves crashed against the side of the boat, like the tail of a thrashing sea serpent trying to knock them into the murky depths. Nicolas looked back at his mother. She clung to François with one arm and with her other hand behind her, grasped the edge of her seat. Sailors bailed water with whatever they could find to keep the boat from sinking. Suddenly, a powerful gust of wind and a wave hit at the same time, tilting the boat. Everybody groped for handholds. It seemed like one of his nightmares as Nicolas turned and saw Simon slide from his seat and disappear into the churning water. His mother gave a high-pitched scream, let go of François, and made a frantic grab for Simon. Nicolas sucked in hard through his nose, and a scream built up deep inside him. Water poured into the boat as he opened his mouth, and his scream exploded into the wind. He glanced down and saw a foot wedged between the boat's side and the top timber for the oarlocks.

"High side!" shouted a sailor.

His mother cried, "Simon! Simon!" as Père Dongé grabbed her arm and François and pulled them to the other side of the boat. While everyone shifted, Nicolas grabbed the foot and pulled. They all ended up in the cold water on the floor of the boat, but it leveled out.

A heavy weight pinned Nicolas to the floor. He gasped for air, and from what seemed a great distance, he heard his mother cry out again. A moment later, he gazed up at her as she lifted Simon off of him. She gathered Simon's motionless body into her arms and wedged herself between two seats so she wouldn't be swept overboard. She clutched him to her breast and rocked back and forth as she wailed. Père Dongé, his eyes filled with a mixture of sorrow and kindness, watched her as he tried to calm François. A sailor attempted to pry Simon from her arms, but she held him fiercely. In the midst of the struggle, Simon stirred slightly, then gagged. His mother leaned him over, and his body quaked as he threw up a bucket of saltwater. "Oh! *Mon Dieu! Merci!* My God! Thank you!" she cried, once again cradling her son like a baby.

Nicolas slumped against a seat as sailors bailed water around him. He drew up his knees and hugged himself, but he couldn't stop shaking. The boat rose on a wave and then headed downward. Nicolas got a closer view of the island. With the name "Massacre," he had expected it to look scary, but not like this! The strong northwest wind made the gray clouds boil just above the treetops, and rain blew in sheets across the land. Trees beyond the beach bent toward the gulf, their limbs performing a ghostly dance. The icy rain felt like pinpricks on his face. All of nature seemed to be shouting, "Beware!"

PIRATES!

In spite of the wind and waves, the bottom of the boat finally scraped shells as the roaring surf propelled it up on the beach. Sailors jumped out and pulled the boat farther ashore. Nicolas scrambled over the side with his bundle. His legs wobbled from being aboard ship for so long and, no doubt, from the experience with Simon.

As sailors helped Nicolas's mother and brothers out of the boat, Père Dongé got his leather bag and Simon's bundle. Then he put his hand under Simon's arm and guided him through the pouring rain. Nicolas carried his mother's basket in one hand and his bundle in the other. As they made their way through the wet sand, Nicolas felt as if weights were on his feet. He barely moved forward, first one leg and then the other. Tall stems of sea oats brushed against his arms as he climbed a sandy, vine-covered slope. Simon stumbled several times, but Père Dongé's support kept him from falling. On the higher ground beyond the beach, the men battled wind and rain as they set up a huge canvas tent. Two-foot-tall bushes covered much of the rugged sandy ground.

Madame La Salle stopped and pointed to some woods beyond the bushes. "Père Dongé, I think we'll seek shelter under those trees."

He looked at the men working on the tent and then at the forest. "Simon is still a little unsteady, so I'll go with you."

Among the large oaks and pines, Nicolas spotted a place where pine needles had fallen on a thick growth of vines. It reminded him of a small cave. Père Dongé went to scout around while Nicolas cleared a place for them to sit within the vines. His mother took a piece of canvas from the basket, and he spread it on the ground. Then they all crawled in and huddled close together. Some water dripped on them from the vines, but they were out of the wind and heavy rain.

When the priest returned, he squatted outside their shelter and said, "This place seems safe, but I'll alert the guard that you're here."

"Merci, thank you, Père Dongé. You are very kind," said Madame La Salle. "I'm sure your help is needed, so we won't delay you longer."

Nicolas's heart sank when he realized Père Dongé wasn't going to stay with them. His face must have shown his feelings, because the priest gave him a reassuring smile and said, "I'll let Monsieur La Salle know your whereabouts. You won't have to stay here long." He hesitated and then stood. He said, *"Au revoir,* goodbye," and walked away.

Their mother said, "Simon, let François lean on you

while I get us something to eat." She turned her back to the younger boys and whispered to Nicolas, "Keep a sharp eye out."

Nicolas nodded. Through the trees and rain, he saw a sailor patrolling with a gun across his arm. Visions of skulls popped into Nicolas's head. His heart raced, and he fought the urge to run to the guard and beg, "Protect me!" But the man would think he was a coward. Nicolas shivered in his wet coat. If he saw anything, the guard and everybody on the island would hear his yell.

Their mother untied a cloth in the basket and passed out rock-hard biscuits. As Nicolas tried to soften one in his mouth, he watched his mother open a glass bottle of vinegar water. Simon and François drank and passed the bottle on to him. "At least this helps to swallow these terrible things," Nicolas mumbled. If only we were in Toulon, he thought. Memories of the city they had left behind in France filled his head—the smell of the salty air, the noisy dock when the harbor was filled with ships, and the three-story houses with shops on the ground floor. He imagined walking past the shops built right up next to the narrow street, and stopping at the bakery. When he opened the door, a warm wave of yeasty, sweet-smelling air washed over him.

"Nicolas!" said his mother. "Are you doing what I asked?"

"*Oui,* Maman." Nicolas looked at the cold, tasteless ship biscuit and swallowed hard to keep back tears.

"Maman, I'm tired," said Simon. "I'll eat this later."

He handed her half a biscuit, put his head in her lap, and was asleep almost instantly.

Nicolas watched his mother stare at Simon as he slept. She absentmindedly rubbed a small mole on the side of her face near her right eye. Out in public, she usually wore a tiny silk or velvet patch glued over the blemish. Some women looked silly, because they wore too many patches. Maman is just as pretty without hers, he thought.

She pulled Simon's *toque* over his ears, smoothed his dark brown hair, and gently patted his face. When she looked up and saw Nicolas watching, she smiled and said quietly, "I'll never forget what you did." Tears welled up in her eyes. "I don't know what I'd have done if . . . ." She wiped her eyes, leaned over, and gave Nicolas a tight hug and a kiss on the forehead. They sat in silence, listening to the wind and rain.

Soon François and his mother dozed as well. Nicolas's head kept nodding, but he'd jerk it up to scan the bushes beyond the trees. Once he thought he saw a slight movement, causing the hair on his neck to shoot up. His muscles tightened, and he barely breathed. But he watched for a long time and didn't see anything else. Finally he deeply inhaled the pine-scented air and relaxed a little. The whistling wind gradually died down, and then the rain stopped.

When his family awoke, his mother said, "Let's move closer to the workers." As they came out of the woods with their wet bundles, the sun appeared. They climbed to the top of a high mound of snow-white sand, spread out the piece of canvas, and sat down to dry in the sun.

When the guard walked by and waved at them, Nicolas began to breathe easier. He lay on his back and gazed at the sky. A spot of blue widened between the clouds. After awhile, he raised up on his elbow. The water, so rough and frightening when they arrived, was now as blue as the sky. Sea gulls called to each other as they glided over the beach. Droplets of water sparkled on brown vines scattered about the white sand dune. All of this, and green pine trees swaying gently in the distance, made the island feel like a different place from earlier that morning.

The large open boat came into the inner harbor after the wind died down, and now sailors unloaded cargo from the *Dauphine* into rowboats. Men carried it from the beach to three tents set up on the high ground. The men reminded Nicolas of ants he'd seen in his courtyard at home in Toulon. Eighty workers had come to the island to construct a warehouse to store cargo. Papa had told him that smaller boats would carry supplies to La Mobile, because the river was too shallow for large ships.

Nicolas lay back on the canvas and thought about Simon's narrow escape. It seemed like a year since that terrible boat ride. He pictured the look in his mother's eyes when she said, "I'll never forget what you did . . . ." I hope Papa will to be proud of me, too. A tiny gray cloud of dread floated across the horizon of his thoughts. What if he blames me for letting Simon slip off the seat?

Nicolas sat up and shook the thought out of his head.

François played in the sand near his mother. Nicolas glanced at Simon just as he threw a tiny shell that hit Nicolas's arm. "Oooh . . . " howled Nicolas, as if he had really been hurt. Simon giggled and threw another. Nicolas hurled it back at Simon, who slid down the dune out of sight.

Their mother frowned and said, "Be careful! You'll put out an eye."

Nicolas wiggled around trying to get comfortable. He had just settled down and closed his eyes when something hit his shoe. He opened one eye and saw Simon sneak around the dune. Grabbing a handful of wet sand, Nicolas waited until Simon took aim with another shell. He flung the sand at Simon's face. The battle was on. Sand and shells flew as the brothers chased each other up one dune and down the next.

Finally Nicolas collapsed on the side of a dune within sight of their mother. Simon flopped down beside him and began to dig in the sand. After a few minutes, Simon asked, "Do you think Governor Iberville is going to die?"

"I don't know," answered Nicolas. "Papa says he's lucky to have lived through the surgery. The doctor cut a hole in his side this big." He held his fingers about six inches apart. "It's a good thing he stayed in the Spanish hospital in Pensacola. He'd never have made it off the ship this morning."

"I hope a doctor never has to cut me open," said

Simon in a low voice.

"You're not the only one," said Nicolas. He lazily watched Simon dig. After a while, a thought popped into his head. He asked, "What if pirates hid treasure on this island?"

Simon's eyes widened. "Do you think they did?"

"They sail up and down this coast all the time."

"How do you know?" asked Simon.

"Sailors talk about it," said Nicolas. When the *Palmier*'s mast was being repaired at Cap-français on Saint Domingue, I walked along the docks and listened to them. One said Governor Iberville took the meanest pirate of all on his first voyage to this land."

Simon frowned. "Why did he do that?"

Nicolas shrugged. "A sailor said the pirates around Hispaniola know this coast better than anybody else."

"The governor wouldn't take a pirate."

"*Mais oui,* but yes, he did," said Nicolas. "His name is Laurens de Graff, but the Spanish call him Lorencillo." Nicolas had a devilish grin as he whispered into Simon's ear, "Do you want to know what he did in Mexico?"

"*Non!* No!" said Simon, pushing him away.

Recalling a neighbor in Toulon who acted out scary stories, Nicolas jumped up. He pretended to hold a sword as he tried to sound like him. "The pirates captured a town and took 150 hostages. They herded the rest of the townspeople into the church and kept them there for four days without food." He flashed the

17

make-believe sword as he acted out the scene. He definitely had Simon's attention. "They broke into houses and took what they wanted." He got right in Simon's face and said in a stage whisper, "But that's not the worst part."

"What is?" squeaked Simon.

Nicolas pretended to roll a barrel. "Lorencillo brought a barrel of gun powder into the church." Nicolas held up his fist and said, "Tell me where you've hidden your valuables, or I'll blow you up!" Nicolas jumped at Simon and yelled, "BOOM!"

"Stop it!" shouted Simon, swinging his arms at his brother.

Their mother stood up and called to them, "What's going on?"

They shook their heads and called back, "Nothin'."

Nicolas sat down beside Simon. "The sailor said 300 people died, but I don't know if they starved or what."

"Did Lorencillo come on *this* island?" asked Simon.

"If he stayed on the ship and didn't come on the island with Governor Iberville, he probably came at some other time. I'm sure he knew about the fresh water ponds that Papa said are on the island."

Simon looked around as if he expected to see Lorencillo behind the next dune. "Do you think the pirates killed the Indians when they came here to get water?"

"You heard what Papa said about the massacre. But he might be wrong," said Nicolas, "and we don't know when the pirates will come back."

From Simon's expression, Nicolas knew his brother heard fear in his voice. So Nicolas bared his teeth at him in another evil grin, trying to hide it.

COMMANDANT BIENVILLE

"I was so scared when those pirates chased our ships," Simon whispered.

"*Oui,* me too," said Nicolas. Just thinking about the pirate ships made his heart beat faster. He glanced at a sand dune in the distance. Did something or someone duck behind it? A shiver ran down his spine as he stared at the mound of white sand. When nothing appeared, he finally pushed the thought out of his mind. He sneaked a look at Simon, then flipped sideways and pinned him to the sand. As his brother squirmed, Nicolas snarled. He made a slashing motion with his finger across Simon's throat. "You're dead, and all the gold is mine!"

Simon let out a blood-curdling scream. He jumped up and ran toward his father, who was heading toward their mother and François.

"What's wrong?" called their father as their mother jumped up in alarm.

In a whiny voice, Simon said, "Nicolas scared me."

Nicolas laughed and fell back on the sand.

His father yelled, "Nicolas, come here!"

"Simon is such a baby," muttered Nicolas to himself. He looked at the sand dune again and sighed with relief as a large sea gull hopped from behind it.

His father scowled at Nicolas and said, "I've got enough problems with our leader too sick to leave Pensacola. I don't need any from you." He looked toward the harbor. "You can help carry supplies. That way you won't have time to pester your brother."

"But Papa!"

His father waved him off. "Bienville will be here at any moment with forty men from Fort Maurepas [MOR eh pah]. I want my first impression to be good— not of a man with unruly children fighting and screaming. I'm the only one who brought his family with him to the island, and I certainly don't want our young commandant to regret it."

Madame La Salle asked, "Do you want me to bring François and Simon to the tent?"

"Stay here and enjoy the warm sunshine," he answered. "I don't know where our quarters will be, but I'll find out and send our trunks when we unload them." He motioned for Nicolas to follow him.

A young man on the beach was shouting orders to three boys about fifteen years old in a rowboat. His dark brown shoulder-length hair flew in all directions as he jerked off his *toque* and shook it at the boys. Nicolas and his father walked down to him, and Monsieur La Salle asked, "Problems, André?"

"*Mais oui,* monsieur!" The young man shook his head

impatiently. "Those cabin boys never do what they're told."

With a slight smile, Monsieur La Salle said, "I'm sure you'll straighten them out." He put a large hand on Nicolas's shoulder and said, "André, you know my son."

"*Bien sûr!* But of course!" With a look of admiration, André tilted his head toward Nicolas. "I saw him save his brother."

His father looked at Nicolas in surprise. "What's this?"

Nicolas shrugged. "I just grabbed his foot and pulled him back into the boat."

"*Au contraire!* On the contrary!" said André, shaking his head. Monsieur La Salle listened in amazement as André made Nicolas sound like a hero as he described what happened.

His father squeezed Nicolas's shoulder and said, "*Mon fils!* I'm proud of you!"

"It was nothing," said Nicolas. But his eyes gleamed.

His father gestured toward André and said, "Monsieur Pénigault [PEN ni go] is one of our best carpenters. He'll help build the warehouse until he's needed to work on a boat." He asked André, "Can you use some help here?"

"*Oui.* There's more work than we can do today."

His father looked straight into Nicolas's eyes and said, "You are at his service. Do whatever he tells you." He put a firm hand on Nicolas's back. "I expect your best." He spoke to some men carrying barrels as he walked slowly toward the supply tents.

André gestured toward some barrels on the beach and said, "You can help Monsieur Minette carry those. They've all got to be moved to the first tent." He yelled to a tall, muscular man, "Philippe, I've got you some help."

The man was carrying something made from two stout poles with rungs like a ladder. He smiled at Nicolas and said, *"Bonjour!* Hello!" as he laid it beside a large barrel. He gestured for Nicolas to help him roll the barrel onto it. "You get between the poles at the front end, and I'll be at the rear. On the count of three, we'll lift. *Un, deux, trois!"* The load was heavy, but Nicolas knew Monsieur Minette was making up for his lack of strength.

Philippe Minette told Nicolas about growing up near Montreal, Canada, as they carried barrels of lard, sugar, and wine. "How old are you?"

"Twelve."

"The same age as Bienville . . . when he joined the French navy," said the man, short of breath as they struggled through the sand. "Do you have brothers and sisters?"

"Two brothers," answered Nicolas.

"Governor Iberville's parents had eleven boys and three girls! But some of them are no longer living," said Monsieur Minette with a note of sadness in his voice. They put the barrel in the tent and walked slowly back to the beach. The man talked about the Le Moynes with as much pride as if he were talking about his own family. He told about Charles, the father, and all his sons who had served France well—such as Iberville, Bienville, Joseph, and Antoine. Then he vividly described their combats at sea, and the Canadian Indian battles Bienville had fought in with his older brothers.

By late afternoon, Nicolas felt as if he'd lived in Canada himself. When the ship from Fort Maurepas sailed into the harbor, Nicolas knew all about Jean-Baptiste Le Moyne de Bienville.

Every muscle in Nicolas's body ached, but the men's excitement about Commandant Beinville's arrival was contagious. Nicolas forgot his weariness as he eagerly watched the commandant come ashore on the first boat. As he came up the beach, a priest walked beside him. Père Dongé hurried toward them, waving and calling, "Père Du Ru!" The two men stopped and waited for him. Père Du Ru introduced Père Dongé to the commandant.

The priests continued to visit as Commandant Bienville moved on, speaking to men along the way. The stocky young man wore a gray-white uniform with blue cuffs on the sleeves, a blue vest, britches, and stockings. The cuffs and lapels of his coat and the rim of his black tricorn hat were decorated with gold braid, and a long row of shiny buttons ran the coat's entire length. Under the hat was a long, curly, wig with the curls pulled to the front.

Nicolas sighed heavily and brushed sand from his blue *capote* as he thought, someday I'm going to have a uniform like that! He looked at the red bows tied in the

commandant's hair, one on each side of his face, and also just below each kneecap. As he got closer, Nicolas saw that his square-toed, black shoes had shiny buckles. A sword hung at his left side, and he carried a half-pike—a metal spearhead with a short shaft.

Since Nicolas's father had spoken of Bienville with such respect, Nicolas imagined the commandant to be about his father's age. He was surprised when he got a close look at him. He asked Monsieur Minette, "How old is he?"

"About twenty-one."

"He's half the age of my father," said Nicolas. "Isn't that young to be a commandant?"

"*Non,* not if you're part of the Le Moyne family of Canada," said Monsieur Minette, his face beaming.

When the commandant got to Nicolas he said, "*Bonjour!* What's your name?"

"Nicolas, monsieur."

"Oh, you must be the son of Monsieur La Salle. I heard your father brought his family. I look forward to meeting him. Does he have you working?"

"*Oui,* monsieur," said Nicolas breathlessly. "I've carried barrels all afternoon."

"*Par excellence!* Excellent! Start early if you want to be a success." He looked at André. "Does he work hard?"

"*Mais oui,* monsieur. He'll make a fine worker in our new settlement."

"*Bon,* good," said the commandant. "We need all the help we can get!" He nodded farewell and went on his way.

"Well, now you've made a good impression," said André. "Keep in his good graces, and you'll have a paying job in a few years."

Nicolas saw a large boy watching them and listening. Creeping out from under his brown *toque* was the curliest red hair that Nicolas had ever seen—and his freckles matched his hair. A tan, medium-sized dog was standing beside him, looking all around. The dog seemed to be trying to figure out the boy's next move. Carrying a small barrel, the boy brushed past Nicholas and said in a low voice, "Commandant Bienville will promise to pay you when he sends you off to live in an Indian village. But will you be around to collect it?" He gave a wicked laugh as he walked away.

AN URGE TO FIGHT

Nicolas felt as if he'd been hit in the stomach. He instantly disliked the boy. He recognized him as one of the boys he'd watched earlier that afternoon rowing in supplies from the *Dauphine*. A dog had been in the boat, and from the boys' gestures, Nicolas decided it probably had shaken water on them. From the beach, he hadn't heard their conversation, but the other boys were obviously mad. One boy had drawn back his fist to hit the red-haired boy, but André had seen them from the shore and yelled at them to stop.

Nicolas wanted a paying job, but not if he had to leave his family and live in an Indian village. His father had told him that on Iberville's second voyage, chiefs from four tribes had invited boys 14 and 15 years old to live in their villages and learn their languages. Six boys were sent so that the French and the Indians could learn to communicate with each other. On this voyage, Iberville had brought twelve boys to learn to be interpreters. Not me, thought Nicolas. War parties raid villages. They kill the men and take women and children as slaves. I don't want any part of it.

A heavily loaded boat landed on the beach. A few minutes later, André shouted to Nicolas, "Here are your trunks." He motioned to the red-haired boy. "Claude, get over here."

Oh, *non,* thought Nicolas, why does it have to be him? Hurrying over to one of the trunks, Nicolas waited impatiently as Claude, with a mocking grin, slowly plodded toward him. His dog followed close behind.

"Need help, runt?" asked the husky boy.

Nicolas grabbed one end of a large trunk and nodded toward the tents. "My father wants it up there."

"Can you carry your part of the load? You look 'bout as strong as a wilting lily," said Claude with a snicker. *"Mais oui.* 'Bout as strong as a wilting lily."

"That's not true," said Nicolas, blushing. "I've worked all afternoon."

"Show me your hands," demanded Claude.

Nicolas held up his free hand. Blisters covered it.

"Bien sûr! Never done a day's work in your life. I've been on my own since I was your age."

Nicolas kept his eyes straight ahead, but he finally asked in a friendly tone, "How old are you?"

"Soon be fifteen," said the boy, proudly.

Nicolas gave him a sideways glance and said, "You look older."

"Mais oui. That's what everybody says." He sniffed and said, "I use it to my advantage too!" He looked Nicolas up and down. "How old are you? Eight?"

Nicolas blushed again and said angrily, "Twelve!"

"You look younger," said Claude. "Much younger!" He shoved the weight of the trunk, almost throwing Nicolas off balance. Giving a loud, mean laugh, he said, "You carry a trunk like you're eight."

Sucking in breath through his nose, Nicolas held it to keep from screaming. He's trying to make me mad, and the more I show anger, the worse he'll get, thought Nicolas. He didn't say anything for a long time.

Claude kept saying, "Cluck, cluck! Cluck, cluck, cluck!"

When Nicolas could stand it no longer, he gave him a disgusted look and asked, "Where were you raised— in a chicken yard?"

Claude wiped his runny nose on the sleeve of his coat then stuck his nose in the air and said, "I was raised in Montreal, Canada, the same place as the great Le Moyne brothers!"

Nicolas looked at him in surprise, but then wished he hadn't. Snot was smeared all over the side of Claude's face. The more Nicolas tried not to look, the harder it was to keep from it. "Does your family . . . still live there?" asked Nicolas, trying to get his mind on something else.

"Maman and Papa are dead," said Claude, wiping his nose on his sleeve again. He glanced up and saw Nicolas staring at him. "What are you looking at?" he snapped.

"Nothin'!" said Nicolas, so fast it made Claude narrow his eyes in suspicion. "I'm . . . sorry . . . to hear about your parents."

"Sorry! Don't waste pity on me. I've been a cabin boy since I was twelve. I stand my own with any drunken sailor. I take care of me!"

"What about brothers and sisters?" asked Nicolas, sneaking a quick glance at Claude's face. He gave a sigh of relief to see that this time the sleeve had done its job.

Claude narrowed his eyes again. "None of your business! And if you don't quit staring at me, I'm going to punch your eyes out of their sockets."

"I'm . . . sorry," stammered Nicolas.

"You're sorry all right! *Mais oui!* You're a sorry good-for-nothing!" Claude let out a roar of laughter.

Again Nicolas fought the fury building up within himself. He's not going to get the best of me, Nicolas thought with fierce determination. He didn't want to give Claude time to think of more insults, so he tried another subject. "Are you going to be an interpreter?"

"Mais oui! I got to be able to talk to the Indians. I'm going to trap beaver and get rich selling their pelts."

"What if a war party captures you?"

"I said I take care of me!"

Nicolas shook his head. I hope you're right, he thought.

Claude pointed to a boy, about seventeen, with the men from Fort Maurepas. "Saint-Michel lived with Indians for two years. Nothin' happened to him. He talks with the people of the Houma tribe almost as good as he speaks French to us."

PROPERTY OF BCC
WALTON COUNTY PUBLIC
LIBRARY SYSTEM

Saint-Michel is really brave, thought Nicolas.

"All Indians sound alike to me," said Claude, "but Saint-Michel says their languages are different. They use the Mobilian trade jargon so they can understand each other."

"What's that?" asked Nicolas. He was surprised when an insult didn't come.

"They don't worry about speaking in sentences— just simple words so they can be understood. The Mobilian and Choctaw languages are similar."

When the boys got to the first tent, Nicolas's father said, "Put the trunk in the center of the tent so it won't get wet if water runs under the sides. These large tents are for supplies, so carpenters are building a lean-to for our family in the woods. I don't know if the smaller tents were left out, misplaced, or if somebody stole them."

On the way to get the second trunk, Claude's mocking tone returned. "Frostbite is gonna' rot off your little toes."

A cold wind blew off the water, but Nicolas felt hot. Claude made him so mad he wanted to knock that slimy nose off his face. But his hand was in no shape to punch anybody. He pulled his coat sleeve over his cold, blistered, right hand. When they got to the beach, Nicolas hurried to the trunk and grabbed the end with his left hand. Claude grinned but didn't say anything.

The boys began carrying the second trunk up the hill. After a while, Nicolas asked, "What's your dog's name?"

"Chienne."

Nicolas frowned. "You just call your dog—dog?"

Claude nodded. "That's what the old sailor who gave her to me called her. I didn't see any reason to change her name after he died." He reached down and petted her head with his free hand. "She's a good hunting dog. I bet you've never hunted."

"*Bien sûr,* I have!"

"You from a city?" When Nicolas nodded, Claude asked, "Where'd you hunt?"

"Out in the country near Toulon."

With a sneer, Claude said, "A big hunter!"

"Have you ever been to Toulon?" asked Nicolas.

"*Non!*" said Claude. "But I've been to La Rochelle with Governor Iberville."

"Well, then you don't know anything about Toulon! I'm probably a better shot than you anyway," said Nicolas. "My father taught me. He explored the Mississippi River with the famous Robert Cavelier de La Salle."

"The one murdered by his own men? Where was your papa then?"

Nicolas stopped and stared at Claude. He wanted to drop the trunk and tear into the larger boy, even if it meant getting beaten black and blue.

Nicolas's father came out from the tent. "Is there a problem?" he yelled.

The boys exchanged glances. Claude called, "*Non.* Just a friendly talk."

"Well, get on up here."

"*Oui,* monsieur," responded both boys. They slowly made their way up the sandy hill and into the tent.

Monsieur La Salle thanked Claude and turned to Nicolas. "Our shelter is in the woods near where you stayed during the rain. Go see what your mother needs from the trunks."

As Claude walked away, he whispered in a baby voice, "Maman! Maman!"

Through clenched teeth, Nicolas muttered to himself, "I'm going to get even with him!"

SOMEONE'S WATCHING

Nicolas didn't realize he'd clenched his hand into a fist until pain shot through the blisters. He shook his hand, trying to dull the pain, as he walked out of the tent and followed the sound of axes into the woods. Men were chopping small pine trees to build the lean-to. Nicolas followed one of them to a place protected by huge oak trees. Their large branches made a kind of roof overhead. Several trees were close together, and the workers leaned the small pines against them to make a sloping roof on one side. Nicolas saw his mother and brothers through the trees. He walked over to them and asked, "What are you doing?"

"Gathering pine straw to sleep on tonight," said his mother. "I'm glad you're here. Take Simon with you to the tent. We need blankets, a water bucket, a cookpot, and a few dishes. Get those, and if I think of anything else you can make another trip."

"*Oui*, Maman, but only two of our trunks are unloaded. I'll see what's in them."

As his mother carried the pine straw to the lean-to,

she said, "Only the blankets are in the trunks. The other things are packed in barrels. Ask your father where they are stored." She frowned as she looked at the blisters on Nicolas's hands. "Find some salve for your hands. It is with my herbs." Nicolas and Simon began the first of several trips to the tent.

The sun set as Nicolas and Simon arrived at the camp with the last supplies for the day. The carpenters finished the lean-to and gathered their axes and tools. A worker said to Madame La Salle, "I'll show your boys how to cut palmetto fronds to cover this. It won't be your house in Toulon, but it'll keep the rain off if we don't have another bad storm." He motioned to Nicolas and Simon to follow him. "Do you have a knife?"

"*Oui,* monsieur!" said Nicolas, proudly. A knife scabbard hung around his neck by a leather strap, and he pulled it from under his *capote.* "Papa gave me this before we left France."

The man led them out of the woods to a slight hill covered with big fan-shaped plants. He demonstrated how to cut the fronds near the ground and watched as Nicolas cut several. "Gather as many as you can before dark," he said, "but be careful. The sides of the narrow leaves will cut you. That's why they're called saw palmetto." He said, *"Au revoir,"* and walked off in the direction of the tents.

Nicolas said to Simon, "I'll cut, and you pile them up. We've got to work fast. The sun has already set."

The palmetto stems were tough, and Nicolas had a hard time cutting them. After a few minutes of working, he stood and stretched while Simon carried several to a clear spot nearby. Suddenly something stirred the palmettos near the top of the rise. It's probably a rabbit, thought Nicolas, as he continued to gaze at the spot. He could have sworn he saw two dark eyes staring back at him. His hair bristled, and a shiver ran down his spine. As he took a step forward, a palmetto frond moved beside him. Nicolas whirled around.

Simon gasped. "What's wrong?"

"Nothin'," said Nicolas, squatting down. His heart raced, but he didn't want Simon to know he was scared. He looked toward where he had seen the movement, but nothing had changed. He went back to gathering palmettos.

"These things are cutting me," complained Simon. "I want to go."

Nicolas stood and handed several fronds to him. "Get a bunch and head for the woods." He hesitated for a moment and then said, "I'm going up a ways to look at something."

Simon begged, "Please go with me."

"It won't take a minute," said Nicolas. He watched Simon slowly drag the palmettos toward the camp. Then he pushed his way through the bushes, breathing rapidly as he neared the spot. There were fewer plants beyond the rise, and dead vines covered a large area. The vines looked flattened, as if something or someone had lain on them. I'm imagining things, he thought. I don't know enough about tracking animals or people to tell anything.

Something white caught his eye in the January twilight. Thinking of buried treasure, he knelt on one knee and dug in the sand with his fingers. They closed around something cold and hard. Nicolas pulled it out of the sand and held it up.

Empty eye sockets stared and hideous teeth grinned at him. Skull! Massacre! He dashed it to the ground and scrambled to his feet. The muscles in his face twitched as he looked around, hoping no one had seen him. He peered at the skull and nudged it with the toe of his shoe. It's too small to be a child's skull, he thought, so it must be some animal. I'm nothin' but a coward— worse than my little brothers. He heard the crunch of shattering bone as he stomped the skull into the ground. No wonder Claude teased me. I deserve it.

Simon and their mother were layering palmetto leaves on the crude shelter when Nicolas returned.

She gestured toward a bed of pine straw in the lean-to. "Sit down and rest, Nicolas." His mother hesitated a moment before she said, "Then I want you to make one more quick trip to gather palmetto."

"It's too dark," whined Simon. "I don't want to go."

His mother looked at Nicolas. "Another armload would keep us warmer tonight. Simon can gather firewood."

François burrowed under a blanket on the pine straw.

"I'm cold," he said.

Nicolas crawled under the blanket with his pudgy little brother. "I'm cold too, and I've never been so tired in my life!"

François snuggled up close and said, "Brrrr . . . ."

Within moments, Nicolas was asleep.

He woke with a start when icy hands closed around the back of his warm neck.

"Feel my cold hands," whispered Simon.

Nicolas flung the blanket back so hard that Simon sprawled out on the pine straw. The look in Nicolas's eyes stopped him before he could call for his mother.

"All right!" said Nicolas, storming out of the lean-to. "I'll go, but I'm not going far." As he went through the woods, he saw men starting campfires. They must be going to roll up in their blankets and sleep beside the fire, he thought. I bet they hope somebody finds their tents.

He went to a clump of palmettos and looked in all directions as he swiftly cut the stems. Light from the campfires flickered in the woods. His hand stopped in midair, and he squinted into the dusk. His heart beat like a war drum as he watched a figure peek from behind a nearby tree.

"Pirates!" shrieked an alarm in Nicolas's head. He gripped his knife and stooped behind a tall palmetto. His mind whirled. How could he sound an alarm with the pirate between him and the woods? His hand shook

so much that he could hardly hold the knife, but he cut the stem and laid aside the frond. With the pirate watching, he'd work as if he didn't know the man was there.

A question wiggled into his thoughts. How do I know it's a pirate? It's got to be. Who else hides behind trees? Indians! His eyes widened as he searched in the growing darkness for paint-streaked warriors. He feared they'd hear his loud heartbeat and mistake it for their drum. The sand dunes were some distance, so except for palmettos, there was no place to hide. His hands felt clammy, and he held his breath as he quietly peeped through and around the clump of palmettos. He slowly let out his breath when he didn't find anyone.

He scanned the tall grass and low dead bushes; he should be able to see anyone lying on the ground there, even though it was almost dark. He stared at the lone tree near the edge of the woods.

It's too late, he thought. They're in the woods ready to attack! They'll kill the men and haul off Maman, my brothers, and me as slaves. He drew in a deep breath, and his muscles stiffened. I'd rather be dead than a slave! He crawled over and got the palmetto fronds to shield himself. He'd hit the warrior in the face with the point-ed leaves and try to knock him off balance as he ran past. Maybe he'd warn somebody.

INDIANS!

As Nicolas leaped from behind the palmettos to charge, he heard André yell, "Claude, get your lazy self over here with that firewood!"

Nicolas, already in motion, sprinted toward the tree. As he ran past Claude, who was suddenly busy gathering wood, Nicolas threw a dry palmetto frond at him and said, "Get your fire off to a quick start."

"Toad-eater!" shouted Claude. "Toad-eater!"

Nicolas laughed as he jogged into the woods. He thought, thank goodness I didn't yell "Indians!" I'd never live that down.

When he dashed into camp, his mother asked, "Where'd you get that energy? I thought you were dead tired."

"I don't know. Maybe from helping a friend."

"I'm glad you've made a friend."

Some friend, thought Nicolas.

Simon, looking skinnier than ever and as tired as Nicolas felt, staggered into camp with an armload of wood and dumped it on the ground.

"I'll start the fire," said Nicolas.

The boys sat near the fire, eating bread and cheese and drinking vinegar water their mother had brought in the basket from the ship. She said, "Try this jerky Monsieur Minette gave us."

Nicolas gnawed on the jerky. "It's not bad. While we carried barrels, he told me how Native people taught him to dry buffalo meat."

"Tomorrow, we'll have a hot meal," said his mother. She pointed to a pot with dried split peas and jerky soaking in water. "He gave me everything I need to cook a stew. In the morning, when the men aren't so busy unloading supplies, I'll get food from the barrels in the tents."

After they finished eating, Nicolas washed his hands again, and his mother put salve on them. Then he and his brothers bedded down in their clothes, wool *toques,* and stockings. Covered with blankets, the pine straw made a fairly soft bed.

Nicolas was almost asleep when his father joined his mother beside the fire. He heard them talking about his rescue of Simon. Pride welled up in him, but his eyelids were too heavy for him to enjoy it for long.

The next morning, Nicolas dreaded leaving the warm blankets. Finally he threw them back, pulled on his shoes, grabbed his *capote,* and dashed out of the lean-to.

His mother was stirring something in a pot hanging over the fire. "Ummm . . . that smells good," said Nicolas.

"Your father brought some cacao beans from the supply tent last night to make *chocolat*," said his mother. Glancing up at him, she asked, "Where's your *toque?*"

"It came off during the night, but it's not that cold," said Nicolas, even though he could see his breath. When his mother gave him a stern look, he went back to get the cap. He jerked the covers off Simon on his way out of the lean-to.

Simon let out a yell, which woke François, who hollered, "Maman! Maman!"

She shook her head. "It *was* a lovely morning."

Simon staggered out, wrapped in a straw-covered blanket. His hair stuck out in all directions from under his *toque.* Grinning slyly, he stood beside Nicolas at the fire.

"What are you up to?" asked Nicolas, suspiciously.

Simon dropped the blanket and stuffed a handful of pine straw down the neck of Nicolas's *capote.*

"Ow! That makes me itch!" Nicolas threw off his *capote* and unbuttoned his vest enough to pull it over his head. Simon laughed and danced around in his blanket as Nicolas pulled his knee-length shirt out of his breeches and shook out the pine straw. "Simon, you'd better watch out!"

"That's what you get for pulling off my blankets."

Their father, carrying several large canes, had walked into the clearing in time to witness the mischief. "That's enough!" he said. "We've got work to do." He laid the canes beside the fire. A hatchet hung from a belt around his coat. He pulled it out and laid it beside the canes. "After you eat, I want the two of you to go across the island to a cane patch." He pointed in the direction from which he'd just come. "The soldier on patrol told me where to find these."

After a breakfast of bread and hot *chocolat,* Nicolas stuck the hatchet in his belt, next to a pouch that hung there. Late yesterday, he had gotten his gloves from the trunk. Now he glanced at his hands as he tied the gloves to his belt. He saw his mother looking at him so he held up his hands. "They look better, but they still hurt."

"Be careful with that hatchet," warned his father. "You can cut yourself so badly that you lose an arm or leg, or die from infection."

"How do we get to the canes?" asked Nicolas.

"Go through the woods," said his father. "When you come out into the bushes and tall grass, you'll see a big mound of shells not far from the water. Past the mound, turn left and you'll see the canes growing along the calm water."

Simon looked from one end of the six-foot cane to the other. "How are we going to get them back here?"

"Nicolas can cut them with the hatchet, then sling them over your shoulder or drag them here. They won't all be that long."

"I can't," said Simon, hanging his head.

"You can! And you will!" said his father.

"Your mother will help lash them together so we can make another room. We'll cover it with mud and make a roof of palmetto like the Native people. That will be the best we can do until we get to the settlement."

"How long will we stay on this island?" asked Simon.

"It'll take a couple of months to get the warehouse built and the supplies moved in," said his father.

"Oh, my goodness!" said their mother. Tears glistened in her eyes. "I hope it's sooner than that."

In the morning light, Nicolas saw dark circles under his mother's eyes, and her face seemed thinner than the day before.

Their father hugged her. "This trip has been hard, but think of the opportunities, Madelaine. You'll be a leading lady in La Mobile."

"I know." She smiled faintly and turned her head, trying to hide a tear trickling down her cheek. "But it's hard being the only lady right now. I miss the three women who were on the ship with us."

"I'm sure you do. I wouldn't want to be the only man with a bunch of women. But when they come from Pensacola in a few weeks, they'll stop here before going to La Mobile." He patted her arm, and she turned and busied herself with the peas and jerky for the stew. His father said to Nicolas, "You made a good impression on Bienville. Prove you're a good worker, and in no time you can earn your own way."

"*Oui,* Papa!" said Nicolas.

"Are you sure it's safe for the boys to go off by themselves?" asked their mother, as she hung the pot of stew over the fire.

49

"The patrols haven't seen any Indians," said their father. "Besides, Iberville and Bienville get along well with them. Chiefs from several tribes including the Mobilians visited them at Fort Maurepas."

Before his mother could speak, Nicolas said, "We'll be extra careful!" Her face showed mixed feelings, but finally she made a shooing motion with her hands.

Nicolas grabbed Simon's coat sleeve and took off. When they were out of hearing distance, he said, "I wanted to get away before Maman told us, 'Don't do this, and don't do that.' I want to explore the whole island. Don't you?"

"Well," said Simon, "I don't want to see any twenty-five foot snakes."

"There are no snakes that big on this island."

"A sailor saw one as big around as his arm."

"Sailors will say anything—especially if they think they can scare you," said Nicolas.

"It's true," insisted Simon. "You just wait and see."

"I will," said Nicolas. They walked through the quiet woods on ground covered with pine straw. The crisp, pine-scented air smelled fresh after yesterday's rain. They heard a sound up ahead and stopped abruptly. After a moment, a squirrel jumped from one limb to the next and disappeared into the branches. Simon let out a nervous laugh.

Finally, the boys came out of the woods. Tall scratchy grass, prickly pear cactus, and palmettos grew in the sandy soil. Up ahead, Nicolas saw a huge mound of shells.

Simon's eyes got large. "Where did all those shells come from?"

Nicolas shook his head. "I don't know, but that's the biggest pile I've ever seen! It looks like a hill of shells." He picked up a shell and examined it as they walked past the mound. They turned left, and when they got nearer the water, he hurled it into the bay.

Up ahead they saw a thick growth of canes on a small strip of land jutting into the water. Most of the tall stalks had brown leaves, but there were a few green ones in the middle of the patch. As the boys got closer, Nicolas saw marsh grass growing in the water beyond the canes. Water gently lapped against the shore.

He gazed across the water that separated Massacre Island from the mainland. Far, far away, the tops of trees were barely visible. Nicolas and Simon walked along the narrow strip of beach, stepping over driftwood and huge logs that had washed ashore. The sand was light brown, not bright white like that on the gulf side of the island. Nicolas thought of the darker sand on the beach at Toulon and felt a tug of homesickness. He'd been so excited about the trip to the new land that he hadn't expected to feel this way. He kicked at the dead grass and driftwood that had washed right up to the cane patch during the storm. He bent down and snapped a stalk of cane. "This breaks, but the hatchet will be faster. I'll cut and you drag it to that clear spot on the beach."

"I want to use the hatchet," said Simon. "I had to drag palmettos yesterday."

"Maybe later. Right now we've got to get some back to Maman, or she'll think we're fooling around. I want to finish early so we can explore."

Simon screwed up his face. "That's not fair."

Nicolas turned his back to Simon, bent over, and hacked the canes. He turned around in time to see his brother stick out his tongue. "Get going!" he yelled.

Simon made a face at Nicolas but gathered the stalks and dragged them away. After a few minutes, he came back with half a stalk, stripped except for two dried brown leaves near the top. He gently flapped the leaves. "Don't these look like donkey ears?"

"Non," said Nicolas. "Get to work."

Simon walked slowly through the narrow path Nicolas had cleared. Still flipping the leaves, he said, "I have to be careful, because donkey's ears stick out so far. I don't want these canes to hurt them." As he dragged off stalks, he said, "Donkey helps me."

"Donkey nothing!" shouted Nicolas. "Hurry up!" His back ached so much that when he stood straight he felt like a bolt of lightning was going through him. When Simon returned, Nicolas handed him the hatchet. "Don't cut your leg."

His brother grinned and attacked the canes with a burst of energy.

Nicolas sat on a log and stripped leaves from the stalks. He'd finished most of them when Simon suddenly stopped cutting.

"What was that?" asked Simon.

"I didn't see anything," said Nicolas irritably. "You're just tired and don't want to admit it."

Simon crept over to him and whispered, "I saw someone in the canes."

Nicolas felt a cold chill pass through his body as he looked at his brother's pale face.

"What'd he look like?" he asked.

Simon trembled as he said in a low voice, "An Indian, and he knows I saw him."

Nicolas tried to build up courage. "Papa said the Mobilians are friends."

"How do we know he's a Mobilian?" asked Simon.

Nicolas's hands gripped the piece of cane in his lap as he gave this serious thought. After a moment, he slowly stood and said, "This is enough. Let's go." He picked up a bunch of stalks and slung them over his shoulder. Simon got the few remaining stalks and rushed ahead of him.

When they were well away, Nicolas looked back toward the shore and asked, "Was it a man?"

"I think so," said Simon, breathlessly.

"Maybe he saw our ship and is curious." Nicolas tried to sound calm. Then he remembered the fleeting glimpse of something ducking behind the sand dune yesterday. He didn't think it was a sea gull. His heart pumped furiously as he visualized himself cutting palmettos late yesterday with dark eyes watching him.

Simon looked over his shoulder. "What if he's mean and others are with him?"

He might be with a war party, thought Nicolas, gasping for air.

When the boys heard voices coming toward them, Simon let out a little yelp, dropped the canes, and dashed into the undergrowth. Nicolas hesitated and then scrambled after his brother.

"LOST SPIRIT"

Moments later, Commandant Bienville and Monsieur La Salle came down the path. "Nicolas is still young, but he's brave and mature," said the boy's father.

"Native people admire bravery," said the commandant. "They say a brave person has a lot of spirit." The two men stopped when they came to the jumble of canes. "What's this?" asked the commandant.

"My sons are gathering canes, but I'm sure they didn't leave these here."

Simon burst from his hiding place. "Papa! Papa! Indians are after us!"

His father looked at Simon in alarm. "Where's your brother?"

Nicolas slowly crawled from under the bushes, though he wished he could stay there forever. His face felt hot, and he was too embarrassed to look at Commandant Bienville.

"Where are they?" asked the commandant.

"I saw one hiding in the canes," said Simon proudly.

"If he was in the canes, why are you hiding here in

the bushes?" asked his father, looking to Nicolas for the answer.

"We heard voices . . . and . . . thought . . ." stammered Nicolas.

"Thought what?" demanded his father.

"It might be a war party," said Nicolas in a feeble voice.

Commandant Bienville coughed. "Monsieur La Salle, it seems that your sons lost spirit this time."

Nicolas had heard Bienville say something earlier about brave men and spirit, so he spoke up eagerly, *"Oui, monsieur!"*

"Well, I hope you're not proud of it!" said his father through clenched teeth.

Nicolas had no idea why his father was so angry. Hesitating, he asked him, "Don't you want me to have lots of spirit?"

His father's eyes bored into him. "Commandant Bienville said 'lost spirit'! You acted like cowards."

Dumbfounded, Nicolas stared at his father.

"Get these canes to your mother!" As his father turned to leave, he said, "I'll take care of you when I get back."

The boys grabbed the canes and rushed along the trail. Simon said angrily, "Papa's going to beat us, and it's your fault."

Nicolas swung around, and the canes on his shoulder almost hit Simon's head.

"It's *your* fault. Besides, I thought the commandant

had said 'lots of spirit.' "

"You can't tell 'lots' from 'lost'!"

Nicolas stuck out his foot and tripped his brother. Canes flew in all directions. In a singsong voice, he said, "Tut! Tut! You *lost* your canes 'cause I got *lots* of brains."

"I'm going to get you!" yelled Simon, as Nicolas ran through the woods with cane stalks bouncing on his shoulder.

François was playing near the lean-to, and his mother was stirring the stew, when Nicolas ran into the camp. He dumped his load beside the lean-to. "I'll be back in a few minutes."

Tears blinded him as he ran out of the woods. When he thought his chest would burst, he dashed behind a sand dune and fell on his hands and knees. Tears dripped from his eyes, and he curiously watched them plop into the sand. After a few moments, he eased his hand under the wet spots. He imagined putting the tears back into his eyes as if they had never come out. If only I could do that with what just happened, he thought. Didn't Papa know how shamed I was in front of the commandant? It wasn't my fault I misunderstood what he said.

As Nicolas relived the scene, he imagined himself saying, "Oh, *non* monsieur, I haven't lost spirit. I'm just protecting it." He said under his breath, "I'll show him I'm not a coward!"

A taunting voice behind him asked, "Is Maman's little boy playing in the sand?"

Whirling around, Nicolas stared up at Claude.

"I'm not playing," he said angrily.

"So, what are you doing?" asked Claude, with his usual maddening grin.

Nicolas grabbed a handful of vines growing on the side of the dune. "I'm looking for the best vines to lash canes for our shelter."

"It looks like playing to me," said Claude. *"Mais oui, it looks like playing to me."*

As Nicolas stood, he glimpsed the three large tents in the distance. "What are you doing over here? The men are way down the beach unloading boats." He gave Claude a piercing look. "You're sneaking away from work—like last night."

Claude jerked his head. "Little do you know! I'm on an errand."

"Bien sûr!" said Nicolas, as he gathered a handful of vines. "No doubt you're about the king's business."

"What do you know about the king's business?"

"My uncles had important jobs in his majesty's service."

"Probably washing his feet," said Claude, slapping his thigh as he let out a loud laugh. "What are they doing now—working in shackles in Toulon? I've heard all about the royal galleys with prisoners rowing the ships. They're nothing but floating prisons."

Nicolas's face turned red. In a low voice, he said, "Both of my uncles died . . . ." Then he added strongly, "But they worked for the Navy like my father."

Claude flipped his hand and said, "Countin' barrels! That's nothin'." He turned and walked off.

Nicolas shook the vines at him and yelled, "You wouldn't eat without those barrels," but Claude didn't look back for a long time. When he finally glanced around, Nicolas pretended to walk slowly in the opposite direction. A moment later, Nicolas ducked behind a dune and watched the husky boy break off a sea oat stem and wave it in the air like a sword as he plodded through the sand. He seemed to be heading toward the woods. Furrowing his brow, Nicolas asked himself, "Why is he going that way at this time of day? None of the men are working over there." When he peeked around the dune again, he saw Claude look in all directions before disappearing among the trees. Maybe he's going to get something from his bedroll, thought Nicolas, but he seriously doubted it. It's strange that his dog isn't with him. To make sure he didn't see Claude again, Nicolas took the long way back to the camp.

His father came into the clearing just as Nicolas arrived from the opposite direction. Simon, looking miserable, sat by the lean-to. His father came straight toward Nicolas and grabbed his arm. "Where have you been?"

Nicolas held up the vines. "I went to see if the vines on the dunes are stronger than the ones growing in the woods. We need them to lash the canes."

"Don't waste time with vines. Get rope from the supply tent." His father jerked his head toward Simon. "Have a seat over there by your brother." He picked out the sturdiest stalk of cane, broke it in half and said loudly, "I came to New France when I was only four or five years

older than Nicolas. I spent years with the great Robert Cavelier de La Salle exploring the wilderness. Now the second day on land my sons prove to be cowards." Simon began to whimper when his father motioned to come to him. Their father's face was scarlet as he grabbed Simon's arm and raised the cane. When his wife rushed into the clearing with François stumbling behind her, he stopped it in midair.

"What's wrong?" she asked. "I heard you shouting all the way into the woods. What have the boys done?"

"Acted like cowards!" roared their father, "and I'm going to teach them what happens to cowards." He raised the cane above his head. Trembling, François wrapped himself in his mother's skirt.

"Cowards!" exclaimed their mother. "Have you already forgotten that Nicolas saved Simon's life yesterday?"

"Stay out of this!" ordered their father, lowering the cane, but still holding tight to Simon's arm. "It was Nicolas's responsibility to keep him in the boat in the first place."

I knew it, thought Nicolas. He always blames me.

Madame La Salle stared at her husband in disbelief. "But only last night you were so proud of him. What has changed?"

"They saw an Indian in the canes, so they ran off like scared rabbits. When they heard voices coming toward them, they panicked and hid in the bushes. They thought Commandant Bienville and I were a war party! I was totally humiliated when my sons crawled out from

61

under bushes."

Their mother tilted her head to one side. "Oh, I see," she said, with a knowing look. "This involves your pride as well as their behavior!"

"They must learn the ways of the wilderness," he declared fiercely. "Native people have no respect for anyone who shows fear."

"Then teach them. Beat them if they willfully disobeyed you. But if they didn't know what to do, teach them."

He glared at his wife for a long moment, then dashed the cane to the ground. "I *hope* you are right, Madelaine." He shoved Simon toward Nicolas and said, "Sit."

Nobody moved for a long time. Eventually, their mother inhaled deeply and slowly exhaled. She gently untangled François from her skirt. Then, with determined steps, she walked over to her husband, put her arms around his waist, and leaned her head on his chest.

He was rigid at first, but after a time he gave a loud sigh and relaxed slightly. He silently stroked her hair as Nicolas counted twenty breaths. Finally, their father said, "I . . . will find ways to teach them." After another long silence, he said to her, "You and François sit with us while I talk to the boys."

Their father dropped heavily to the ground as if he were tired to the bone. He stared in the distance for a while. Then he looked from Nicolas to Simon.

"Think before you act, or you'll get yourself killed. If you must hide, don't move."

"But Papa . . ." Simon interrupted.

"Keep silent!" he ordered. "Don't leave evidence. Canes scattered helter-skelter on the trail would alert a blind man. Only the keenest observer knows when a warrior has passed that way." As he took a deep breath, he looked Nicolas directly in the eyes. "Do you know how the Mobilian tribe teaches their children to overcome fear?" When Nicolas shook his head, his father continued. "André and some other men were in a Mobilian village a few years ago. They witnessed a festival that's held each September. Everybody, from youngest to oldest, gathers in the village plaza. The children are flogged until blood comes."

Simon's voice quavered as he asked, "Why?"

"The chief and old men explain to the children that this teaches them not to fear the evils their enemies can do to them," answered his father. "It makes them good warriors that never cry out or shed a tear. Warriors and even women can be burned alive and never make a sound."

"What if the child is sick?" asked their mother.

Their father hesitated before he answered. "Then the mother is flogged instead."

She bowed her head. "This place is too cruel. How will we survive?"

With a look of determination, her husband said, "If the Le Moyne family survived fierce Canadian winters, we can certainly make it here. Madelaine, I'm proud you're brave enough to come with the boys and me. I'm sure Governor Iberville wishes his wife were with him instead of in France."

Nicolas watched his mother stand and smooth her clothes. She stared at the crude lean-to. With a forced smile, she said, "I'll try to remember the grand dreams we had for life in this new country. In the meantime, I'll make this place livable. Come with me, François."

"Madelaine, you've got lots of spirit," said their father before she turned to leave. His eyes reflected his admiration as he watched her disappear into the lean-to. He glanced at Simon, but he looked into Nicolas's eyes as he said to both boys, "There are hard, hard lessons to learn in the months ahead, if you are to become brave, trustworthy young men." An expression of hope covered his face as he said, "I know my sons will live up to my expectations."

Nicolas thought, What if . . . I don't? What if . . . I can't? He felt as if the twenty-five-foot snake that Simon talked about had wrapped itself around him.

THE THIEF

Simon wrinkled his brow and asked, "Why was the Indian hiding in the canes?"

"Most likely, he knew we were coming," said his father. "No French women or children have come on Iberville's other voyages, so maybe he wanted a closer look without frightening you."

"He did anyway," said Simon.

His father smiled. "What would you have done if he had walked toward you?"

"Screamed and run away!"

"If the man on patrol had heard you scream, he'd have thought you were in danger and might have shot the man. The Mobilians are people like you and me. They want to be friends."

"How would he know we were coming?" asked Nicolas, trying to forget about his father's expectations.

"According to Iberville, the Pensacola tribe that now lives on Mobile Bay has good relations with the Mobilian tribe. They pass along information to each other. We saw the Indians that hunt game for the

Spanish at Santa Maria de Galve come and go. Since we stayed there almost three weeks, word had time to spread."

"There isn't a village here on the island, is there?" asked Nicolas.

"Not now. There was one several years ago . . . ." His father's voice trailed off, as he twirled a pine needle between his fingers. "When Iberville and his men found the skeletons, they also found what they think was the remains of a village."

Nicolas asked, "So where did the Indian come from?"

"I imagine some families came to the island to get oysters," said his father. "From the piles of oyster shells around here, somebody is eating them."

"*Mais oui!*" said Simon. "That's a huge pile near the water. But where's his family?"

"They probably went back to the mainland before the storm, or they might be hiding on the island. However, you are the only ones so far to see an Indian."

"You said the Mobilians want to be friends," said Nicolas. "Did you make friends when you explored the Mississippi River?"

"*Bien sûr,*" said his father. "As we went downstream, village chiefs gathered and sang the calumet of peace to show they wanted peace and friendship."

"What's a calumet?" asked Nicolas.

"A stick or hollow cane. It's decorated with feathers, and a pipe is on the end of the cane stem." Their father placed his hands together and fanned out his fingers.

"The feathers tied together around the stick look similar to several ladies fans joined together."

Nicolas asked, "Why do you say 'sing the calumet of peace,' if it is a cane?"

"Singing is an important part of the ceremony, and depending on the tribe, they might dance and smoke the peace pipe. Iberville isn't a smoker, but he takes a few puffs to show respect for the native customs. I'm sure when he gets here area chiefs will gather for the three-day ceremony."

Simon asked, "When will that be?"

His father shrugged. "We might be at the new settlement before he's able to come."

Monsieur La Salle stood and brushed pine straw from his clothes. "I've got to get to work so the men can build the warehouse. I want you to gather more canes."

When Simon gave Nicolas a questioning look, Nicolas asked their father, "What do you want us to do if we see an Indian again?"

He answered with a question. "Do you like to give something to a new friend?" The boys nodded. "Come with me to the tent, and I'll get some trinkets—maybe a mirror and a comb." As they walked through the woods, he said, "If you see an Indian watching, go on with your work. He knows you've seen him. After a few minutes, look in his direction and smile. Before you take the canes to our camp, hold out a trinket to let him know you want to give it to him. Leave it where he can easily get it. Before long, you'll be friends."

They heard a noise at the workers' camp up ahead, so their father signaled the boys to stand still. After a moment, he gestured that he was going to circle around to the other side of the camp. He whispered, "Talk loudly as you walk through the woods."

Nicolas whispered to Simon, "Let's pretend to quarrel." Nicolas sounded mad as he said in a loud voice, "It wasn't my fault we got into trouble. If you hadn't dumped the canes on the trail, none of this would have happened."

Simon followed his lead. "You tripped me! That's why I dropped them."

"And I'll do it again," said Nicolas. He stuck out his foot, and Simon almost fell.

"*Mais non,* you won't!" yelled Simon, regaining his balance. He hit Nicolas on the back.

They stopped acting when their father, holding Claude's arm in a tight grip, appeared on the path ahead of them. The boy's face was bright red.

"I caught him going through a worker's trunk," said their father. "He let a trunk lid fall, which made the noise we heard." He narrowed his eyes and said to Claude, "You probably went through others, too, since I saw you moving away from another trunk."

"I didn't steal anything," said Claude. "You can search me."

"I'll let the commandant do that."

Nicolas and Simon followed as their father led Claude to the tents. Now I understand why he didn't have his dog with him, thought Nicolas. It serves him right to

get caught. He's such a bully.

Commandant Bienville was talking with André outside the tents. André frowned at Claude and said, "In trouble again, are you?"

"What's he done now?" demanded the commandant.

"I caught him going through a worker's trunk," said Monsieur La Salle.

"He's constant trouble," said André. "If he's not hiding to avoid work, he's sneaking around like a thief. He almost got in a fight yesterday."

"Search me! It'll prove I didn't steal anything," said Claude, in a self-confident tone.

With an angry jerk of his head, the commandant indicated to André to search the boy. "I thought my brother, Iberville, made a mistake when he agreed to take you on as a cabin boy. He only did it out of respect for your late father."

André shook his head when he didn't find anything on Claude.

Monsieur La Salle said, "Perhaps he hid the goods and plans to get them later."

"*Non!*" Claude said, defensively. "I'm not a thief."

"Unfortunately, that's not what your older brother thinks," said Commandant Bienville.

"He's the thief!" shouted Claude. "He stole the inheritance my mother left me!"

"He has a different story," said the commandant sharply, "but that's between you and him. Why were you rummaging through a trunk, if you weren't stealing?"

Claude shrugged. "What a man keeps in his trunk tells a lot about him. I like to know all I can about the men."

The commandant looked at him suspiciously. "Why? You wouldn't stoop to . . . ." Before he finished, a worker ran up to tell him that an accident had happened on the beach. Grabbing Claude by the arm to take him along, he turned to follow the worker. He called back to Monsieur La Salle, "I'm going upriver in a few days, and he'll go too."

Nicolas almost felt sorry for him when Claude said again, "I didn't steal anything!"

Monsieur La Salle called after the commandant, "With your permission, I'll give my boys a few trinkets in case they see the Indian again." The commandant nodded vigorously as he rushed off with Claude and André.

Their father gave them a small mirror and a comb. "Remember what I've told you, and be careful with the hatchet."

"*Oui,* Papa," said the boys. On their way back to the cane thicket, they saw the two priests and a carpenter in the woods.

Père Dongé smiled warmly and called, "*Bonjour!* Where are you boys going?"

"To the cane thicket across the island," replied Nicolas.

"We're gathering canes," said Simon, "and I saw an Indian man hiding in them."

"Don't worry," said Père Du Ru. "I've been in La

Louisiane for two years now, and I've gotten to know lots of Native people. He won't hurt you."

"What are you doing?" asked Nicolas, wondering why the men were standing in the woods.

Making a sweeping gesture with his arm, Père Dongé said, "We're selecting a tree to make a large cross like the one Père Du Ru made at Fort Boulaye. I want to learn all I can from him before he returns to France."

"Where's Fort Boulaye?" asked Nicolas, in no hurry to return to the canes.

"It's up the Mississippi River," said Père Du Ru. "Did you know Bienville was commandant there before he took over at Fort Maurepas?" The boys shook their heads.

"When are you going back to France?" asked Nicolas. In case I want to go with you, he thought.

"Whenever Governor Iberville is ready and able— probably in April."

"When you get all the canes you need, will you gather some for us?" asked Père Dongé. "I want Père Du Ru to show me how to build an altar from them."

"*Oui,* monsieur," said Nicolas. "We'd better go." He wanted to stay and watch the men cut the tree, but his father expected the canes to be cut. The word "trust-worthy" kept echoing in his mind. If I can't be brave, he thought, at least I can try to be trustworthy. Nicolas said, *"Au revoir,"* and he and Simon went on their way.

As they passed the shell mound, their pace slowed. They looked in all directions before they started along the narrow beach. The driftwood, the marsh grass, the cane thicket—everything that had looked so peaceful and calm earlier in the morning now seemed frightening.

Simon walked so close behind Nicolas that he stepped on his brother's heel.

When Nicolas glared at him, he whispered, *"Pardon,"* but he still stayed near. Nicolas stopped and looked at the place where he had earlier cut the canes. Simon peered into the thicket and whispered, "I'm scared."

Nicolas's hands shook as he began chopping with the hatchet. When Simon whispered, "I'm scared!" for the hundredth time, Nicolas shouted, "Simon!" His little brother jumped a foot high and tears trickled down his cheeks. In a low voice, Nicolas said, "Work fast!"

They carried a load of canes to the camp without seeing the man. While there, they ate some of Monsieur Minette's stew, as they called it since he'd given them the ingredients. It wasn't the best stew Nicolas had eaten, but it was hot.

The boys were less nervous after their third trip and still no Indian. Nicolas whacked canes until late in the afternoon. He said, "This is enough to satisfy Papa."

When Simon suddenly gasped, Nicolas looked up in time to see the dark outline of a person just before the cane stalks came together and hid him. Nicolas whispered, "You know what Papa said, so keep working." He took the mirror from his pouch, looked at himself, and wiped a smudge from his face. Even though he couldn't see anyone in the canes, he smiled and looked into the mirror again. He put it back into the pouch and finished his work. He said in a calm voice, "Simon, take as many stalks as you can carry, and I'll get the rest." Nicolas laid the mirror on a nearby log. "Now, we'll see if it works." When he glanced back, the canes were swaying, even though there was no wind—as if a ghost were silently moving through them.

A STRANGE ENCOUNTER

Nicolas and Simon were well down the beach before they gathered the courage to stop and look back. Nicolas, surprised to see someone already standing beside the log, stared in amazement. The Indian had his back to them, but when he glanced around, Nicolas said, "Why, he's only a boy . . . about my age." He was wrapped in an animal–skin robe that hung down to his knees, but his legs and feet were bare. He picked up the mirror and looked into it, but Nicolas couldn't see his expression. Then he quickly disappeared into the canes. I want to become friends, thought Nicolas, so I can learn his language without having to live in his village. He took a deep breath, and a smile covered his face. "It worked!" he exclaimed, doing a quick little dance step up and down, to and fro.

The boys raced to the camp with the canes.

"Papa! Maman!" yelled Simon.

Their mother and father, busy attaching palmetto fronds to the lean-to, jerked around. "What now?"

asked their father, his voice a mixture of alarm and irritation.

"We saw a boy!" shouted Nicolas, before Simon could answer.

"I wanted to tell!" Simon dumped the canes and kicked them, causing them to clatter all over the ground.

"Shoo!" His mother put her finger to her lips. "François is asleep."

In a low voice, Simon said, *"Pardon,* but that's not fair. Nicolas tells everything!"

"So *you* tell me what happened!" exclaimed his father.

With less eagerness, he said, "I saw the boy in the canes, so Nicolas laid the mirror on a log, and he came and took it."

"So it's a boy, instead of a man," said their father. "How old is he?"

With enthusiasm, Nicolas said, "About my age or a little older."

"He'll be back!" said their father with confidence.

Their mother looked at him in surprise. "You *want* him to come back?"

"Mais oui!" The boys can help us build a friendship with his tribe, which no doubt is Mobilian." Their father's eyes reflected his high hopes as he said to Nicolas and Simon, "You can learn his Mobilian language. The Mobilian Jargon—simple words from several languages—is based on it."

"Claude mentioned that," said Nicolas, remembering

that the boy had answered his question about that without his usual insults.

"Native people from the Atlantic to the Mississippi River can understand it," said their father. "That's why it's so important for you to learn it."

Nicolas coughed and tried to relax the muscles in his face, but his eyes betrayed him. His mother, who had been watching him, said firmly, "Our sons are not going to be interpreters. They're too young."

"Well, not right away," replied their father. He looked directly at Nicolas. "The fastest way to learn a language is to live with the people, so you speak it every day. I learned some Iroquois when I was traveling with Monsieur Cavelier de La Salle in New France, but I didn't spend enough time with any other tribe to learn their language."

Simon stepped closer to his mother. "I want to stay with you."

She gave him a hug. "And that's what you're going to do!"

Nicolas breathed easier when his mother turned to the evening meal and the conversation changed to other things.

It was so cold that night that Nicolas even wore his *capote* to bed. Snuggling under the blankets, he thought about the Indian boy. I'll ask him if he'd seen a mirror before. I'll make him understand by making signs with my hands.

Soon everybody was asleep except Nicolas. Bright moonlight shone around the blanket hanging over the open side of their shelter. He stared at the palmetto fronds covering the lean-to and listened to Simon's steady breathing. Hearing a plop on his blanket, he thought a piece of bark had fallen, so he brushed it off. He was startled to see it fly over to Simon. Nicolas raised up on his elbow and watched a bug as long as his thumb, crawl up his brother's shoulder. It looked similar to a cockroach. When it started to crawl across Simon's face, Nicolas had a powerful urge to scream. But his father would be furious if he woke the family. Simon looked so funny wrinkling his nose in his sleep that Nicolas put his hand over his own mouth to keep from laughing. Still asleep, Simon swatted his face, knocking the bug off. Nicolas looked down but didn't see it. Suddenly he felt it inside the neck of his coat. He went from his propped-up position to a wild wiggly dance in a split second. Squirming out of his coat, he hopped from one foot to the other and stifled the "Yaaaaaaa!!!" that was rising in his throat. He stomped the bug and heard a "pop" as its guts squished out.

As his father turned over, Nicolas dove under the blankets. "What's wrong?"

"Nothin', Papa," said Nicolas, stuffing his coat under the blanket. He didn't move until he heard his father snoring. As he quietly put on his coat, he saw the flattened cockroach in the moonlight. "I'm going to save it and tease Simon later," he said to himself, pushing it under some pine straw.

The next morning, Nicolas was up before his parents, even though it was freezing. He gathered extra firewood and built up the fire. He knocked the thin layer of ice out of the bucket and got fresh water from the barrel well the sailors had dug in the sand. A fire was blazing when his mother came outside.

"You're up early this morning," she said.

"I want to get started, so we can build another shelter." Nicolas gestured toward the lean-to. "It's too crowded in there." Trying to avoid a discussion with his mother about the Indian boy, he said, "I'll wake Simon so we can eat and get to work."

After breakfast the boys took off for the cane patch. When they were almost out of the woods, Nicolas felt his pouch.

"What's in there?" asked Simon.

"In where?"

"I saw you feel something in your pouch."

"Just a little piece of a mirror," said Nicolas. "That was probably the boy's first time to see one. Since I can't ask him, I brought a mirror to use with hand signs."

Simon smiled. "I'll make donkey ears and ask him if he's seen any donkeys."

"Are you slow-witted? There aren't any donkeys around here."

Sounding cross, Simon asked, "How do you know?"

"Have you seen any?"

"No. I've only seen squirrels and birds," said Simon.

"That doesn't mean other animals aren't here. I heard sailors talking about raccoons, buffalo, and . . . ."

Nicolas stopped on the trail. "You're right. There are other animals around here." He gave Simon a sly grin. "And I know a secret about one."

"What's the secret?" whispered Simon.

"If I tell you, it won't be a secret."

"Please!"

Nicolas motioned for him to come close. He opened the pouch hanging from his belt and carefully took out the squashed bug. "Do you know what this is?"

"Bien sûr," said Simon. "It's like a cockroach. And a big one! I saw some in Pensacola. So what's the secret?" When Nicolas rolled his eyes and looked at the sky, Simon demanded, "Tell me!"

"I saw it run across your face last night!"

"YOU DID NOT!" yelled Simon.

In a teasing voice, Nicolas said, "Yes, I did!" He threw the bug at him, then dashed out of the woods and through the tall grass toward the water's edge. Simon squealed and chased him, jumping over driftwood and rotten logs. Nicolas ran into the cane patch and ducked behind some thick growth.

Simon screamed, "Come out, Nicolas. That's not fair!"

"Come and get me, chicken. Cluck! Cluck!" Nicolas silently stepped back.

"I will! Just watch!" Simon pushed his way into the canes.

80

Nicolas took several quick steps backward. Then he hollered as he stumbled, crashed through cane stalks, and landed on his bottom with his legs sprawled over a big log. He was dumbfounded when he realized he'd fallen backward into a dugout canoe. The boy in the canoe looked just as startled. Nicolas scrambled out and watched the canoe back silently into the water.

"Wait! Wait!" he yelled. "Don't leave!" He motioned for the boy to come back, but the canoe glided out of sight around a bend. Nicolas stomped out of the cane patch. "I scared him away!" he yelled.

"HUSHI HUMMA"

"I could kick myself," said Nicolas, brushing dirt off the back of his *capote.*

"What happened?" asked Simon, walking toward Nicolas from a short distance down the beach.

"The boy we saw yesterday had pulled his dugout canoe into the canes, and like a slow-wit, I fell backward into it."

"What did he do?"

Nicolas glared at Simon and said, "He stared at me, and I stared at him. What do you think?"

"I thought an Indian had attacked, until I heard you yelling, 'Wait, wait! Don't leave!'" Simon put his hand on his hip and said, "So you just sat in the canoe staring at each other?"

"*Non!* I got out of there as fast as I could. Where were you when I needed you?"

Simon smiled sheepishly. "When all the crashing and hollering started, I lost spirit and beat a path down the beach."

Nicolas frowned. "I should have known."

Simon ignored him and asked, "Do you think he watched us all night?"

"I don't know. Maybe he was fishing or gathering oysters. He'll probably come back. In the meantime, we've got to work."

The boys worked about half an hour before Simon silently pointed toward the canes near the water. Nicolas saw them move slightly. "He's back," Simon whispered excitedly. "I have two biscuits in my pouch. I'll eat one and leave one for him."

"It's worth a try," said Nicolas. He continued to hack cane.

Simon sat on a log in the sun and pretended to enjoy chewing the hard biscuit. He held a short piece of cane with two dead leaves on the end. He flipped the leaves several times.

Nicolas came and sat down beside him. "You're too old to play like those leaves are donkey ears. That's for François." When tears welled up in Simon's eyes, Nicolas said, "Never mind. Do whatever you want."

"This is for our new friend," said Simon, glancing toward the canes as he flipped the leaves again. He said softly, "Donkey ears remind me of home. Remember the donkey that pulled the old man's vegetable cart down our street in Toulon?" Nicolas nodded. Simon said, "I talked to the man almost every day. He never said, 'Go away! I'm busy.' I petted the donkey. It was soft and warm. I want to go back to France and live in our three-story house—not in the woods with cockroaches crawling across my face!" Tears spilled down his cheeks.

Nicolas put a firm hand on Simon's back and said, "I know, but don't let the Indian boy see you cry." Nicolas leaned forward with his hands between his legs and stared at the ground. He knew exactly how his brother felt.

Simon sniffed a few times and said, "It scares me for Papa to talk about you and me living in an Indian village to learn their language."

"Me too," said Nicolas. "But if we make friends, we can learn it from this boy without living with him." They stared at the still figure now only partly hidden. He was wrapped in the same animal skin as the day before. "He knows we see him." Nicolas pulled off his *toque* and took the comb out of his pouch. His long, tangled hair was hard to comb. When he finished, he laid the comb on the log and put the *toque* on again. "You leave the biscuit, and I'll leave the comb."

They took some cane stalks and went far enough down the beach so the boy would feel safe, sat down on a huge log, and began to strip leaves from the stalks. In a few minutes, the Indian boy cautiously moved out of the canes. The boy's robe flapped open as he moved, and Nicolas saw a long piece of leather that evidently went between his legs and folded in the front and back over a narrow strip of leather around his waist. It looked like a small leather apron. He'd seen Indians at the Spanish settlement in Pensacola dressed like this. A leather pouch also hung from the strip.

Simon shivered as he looked at the boy's bare feet and legs. "Isn't he freezing?"

Nicolas shrugged. "I guess he's used to it. With the sun out, it'll soon warm up."

The boy picked up the biscuit and smelled it. He tried to break it, but it was too hard. He made a face and threw it into the water. Simon laughed and clapped his hands. The boy, surprised by Simon's outburst, began to jump away but then hesitated.

Simon yelled, "That's what I think of those biscuits, too." He made a face and pretended to throw a biscuit into the water. The boy smiled faintly and picked up the comb. He turned it over in his hand. Then he carefully tried to pull it through his coarse black hair. He winced several times but finally managed to get it all combed. Simon clapped again and yelled, "Comb! Comb!" He pretended to comb his hair. "Comb." They saw the boy's lips move as he tried to say the word to himself.

Nicolas got out the piece of mirror. He waited until the boy looked at him, and then he looked into the mirror and smiled. He pointed to himself and said in a loud voice, "Nicolas." He continued to look in the mirror as he took steps toward the boy.

Simon walked even closer as he pointed to himself and said, "Simon. Simon." He pointed to his brother and said, "Nicolas." They watched with wide eyes as the boy pushed back the robe and opened the pouch hanging from his waist. Simon whispered, "He's almost naked in this cold weather!" Nicolas elbowed him as a warning to be quiet.

Pulling out the mirror they'd left for him yesterday, the boy looked at himself, pointed to his chest, and said something in a low voice.

Nicolas repeated his own name and pointed to himself. Then he pointed to the boy, who smiled timidly but shook his head. Nicolas put his hand behind his ear as a sign that he hadn't heard him. The boy pointed to himself and again shook his head. "He understands," said Nicolas, "but for some reason he doesn't want to tell us."

Simon pointed to the boy and said, "No Name. Your name is No Name."

The boy furrowed his brow and said, "Na No."

"No! No! No!" shouted Simon, shaking his head. "Your name is No Name."

"No! No! No!" said the boy, shaking his head in perfect imitation of Simon.

Simon clapped and laughed. Then he moved his lips very slowly and said, "No Name."

Scrunching his lips together like he was kissing the air, the boy said, "No. No. Na." Simon shook his head helplessly.

"Let me try," said Nicolas. He moved several steps closer to No Name. He pointed to the boy and said, "No."

"No!" responded the boy eagerly.

Nicolas pointed to him again and said, "No Name. No Name."

"No Nay! No Nay!" No Name smiled proudly.

Nicolas smiled and tried again. "Nay . . . mmm . . . ."

"Nay . . . uuum."

Nicolas nodded encouragement. "That's better." They spent the next few minutes repeating their names as they pointed toward themselves. No Name tried his best to say "Nicolas," but they finally settled for "Nick." He sounded like a hissing snake when he tried to pronounce "Simon."

Suddenly, Nicolas remembered their task. He said, "Go," and pointed toward the trail to the woods. He made motions for No Name to go with them, but the boy shook his head. When Simon and Nicolas hauled off the stalks of cane, No Name watched them for a long time. Then he turned and walked toward the shore.

"Do you think he will come back?" asked Simon as he dragged his canes through the woods.

"I hope so," answered Nicolas. "He's the only thing that will keep us from being sent off to live in an Indian village without Maman and Papa."

Their mother was washing the cookpot when Nicolas and Simon dumped the canes near the lean-to. In a fast high-pitched voice, Nicolas said, "We saw the Indian boy again."

Simon's excitement bubbled out as he said, "We tried over and over to teach him our names. He sounds like a snake when he tries to say 'Simon.'"

Simon made hissing sounds until Nicolas interrupted.

"We're going to tell Papa!" They were off before their mother could protest.

"I'm going to tell him," said Simon. "You told Maman."

"Not if I beat you there." Nicolas took off like an arrow shot from a bow. He heard Simon screaming at him, but he kept running. Finally, he ducked behind a sand dune and waited. When he heard Simon sniffling and fussing to himself, Nicolas quietly circled the dune. He let out a screech, rushed Simon from behind, lifted him off his feet, and swung him around, letting him fall in the sand.

"Leave me alone!" yelled Simon.

Nicolas pulled him to his feet. "Come on. I'll let you tell Papa."

Their father and Commandant Bienville, looking disturbed, were bent over a barrel when the boys rushed into the tent. Nicolas asked his father, "What's wrong?"

"Another keg of spoiled bacon. I don't know what we're going to do."

Commandant Bienville said, "We'll make out, because we can trade with the Mobilians for corn."

"We saw a Native boy this morning," said Simon, his eyes sparkling. He pointed to his forehead and said, "His head was sort of flat. Was he Mobilian?"

The commandant nodded and said, "Or Choctaw."

"Was he the same person you saw yesterday?" asked their father.

Simon nodded. "We talked to him too. We told him

our names, but he didn't say his loud enough for us to hear. So I called him No Name."

The commandant smiled and said, "He probably is Mobilian. Native people around here don't like to tell their names."

"Why?" asked Nicolas.

He shrugged and said, "I don't know. It's just the custom. He'll let a friend tell you, but he won't."

"Well, I guess we'll have to use No Name then," said Simon.

"Are there other things like that we should know?" asked Nicolas.

The commandant put his hand on his chin and thought for a moment. "They don't like to mention the names of the dead. Of course, you won't have any reason to ask about dead family members." As he moved to the next barrel, he added, "I want to talk to him if he comes back."

"Can you speak his language?" asked Nicolas.

"Enough to communicate," he said, opening the lid of the barrel. "Fortunately, 1 learn languages easily, so I can talk with several tribes."

"We're busy, so you boys get back to cutting canes," said their father.

"We'll let you know if we see the boy again," said Nicolas. *"Au revoir."*

The boys wasted no time in crossing the island. No Name sat on the log near the water looking into the mirror. They knew he heard them coming, but he didn't make a move to run away. He stood as they slowly walked toward him. He motioned toward the canes, asking with hand signals if they were going to cut more. Nicolas nodded. No Name pointed toward the hatchet and then toward himself and pretended to whack. Nicolas hesitated. He wasn't afraid No Name would hurt them, but he didn't know if his father wanted someone else to use the hatchet. No Name's eyes seemed to question his trust. Finally Nicolas pulled the hatchet from his belt and handed it to him. The boys watched in amazement as he swiftly cut the canes. Soon there was a large pile.

Nicolas and Simon quickly stripped the leaves and began to gather the canes. Nicolas motioned with his hands, asking if No Name wanted to carry some. The boy picked up a large bunch and easily slung them over his shoulder.

The three boys walked through the quiet woods with the canes slapping against their shoulders. When they came into the clearing, No Name pointed at the lean-to and said, *"Itta bena."*

"What?" asked Simon, putting his hand behind his ear.

No Name slowly said each syllable. *"IT-tah BEE-nah."*

Simon said, "Itty bitty."

No Name smiled, shook his head, and repeated the word.

Simon tried again but didn't do much better.

He said, "That's our house." He pointed to the lean-to and said, "House."

No Name said, "Hoose."

Since their mother and François were not at the camp, the boys went off to find Commandant Bienville. No Name followed. They heard hammers long before they saw the carpenters building the large wooden warehouse. The commandant was talking with his brother Antoine, supervisor of the construction.

André was nearby watching three men work. One man stood on a platform made from two high sawhorses with boards across them, and two men were below him. Together they worked a large saw to cut a log.

The boys walked up behind André, and Nicolas asked, "What are they doing?"

Without taking his eyes off the workers, André said, "Cutting a beam for the warehouse with that framed pit saw." When he turned toward the boys and saw No Name, a big grin covered his face. He spoke to the boy in a language Nicolas didn't understand and then hollered, "Commandant, look who's here!"

When the commandant saw No Name, his eyes lit up, and he hurried over. He held out his hand as he spoke to the boy in the language André had used.

No Name took the commandant's hand and squeezed gently as he leaned his head slightly toward him. The boy said, *"Chishno pisah yukpah siah it tikana su."* (I am glad to see you my friend.)

The boys tried to follow the conversation and hand

motions. Several times No Name pointed to them. When they paused, Nicolas said to the commandant, "You must know him."

"Mais oui!" said Commandant Bienville. "About two years ago when I explored Mobile Bay and up the Mobile River, I met Red Bird's family. His father is *mingo,* (headman or chief) of a small Mobilian village."

"His name is Red Bird!" exclaimed Simon.

"'Hushi Humma' means 'Bird Red,' or as we say, Red Bird. His mother saw one when he was being born."

"What language were you speaking, and what did you say to him?" asked Nicolas. "All I got from your signs was something about a boat."

"It was Mobilian jargon, and I said I planned to visit his village in a few days. Red Bird's father learned from the Indians in Pensacola that our ships were there and that we would be coming here. Several families have been on the island gathering oysters, but they went back to the mainland before the storm. Red Bird wanted to be able to tell boys in the village that he saw us first, so he came back when the weather cleared. He watched you and Simon carefully before he let you see him."

"Oh," said Nicolas, sighing with relief. "That explains some things."

The commandant laughed. "You mean you thought you saw something, but when you blinked and looked again, there was nothing there?"

Nicolas nodded. "*Oui,* monsieur."

"I hope someday I'll be able to see as keenly and conceal myself as well as these warriors. We think our ways are superior, but we have much to learn . . . if we are willing."

I'm willing, Nicolas said silently. The thought surprised him. But he promised himself—I *will* watch and listen. I might not be brave, but I'm smart. Maybe even smart enough to solve the mystery of the massacre—to find out what really happened.

ALLIGATOR ATTACK

Nicolas asked, "What does IT-tah-BEE-nah mean?"

Commandant Bienville looked at Red Bird, who leaned his head toward Nicolas and Simon and spoke a few words. "It means 'house in the woods,'" said the commandant. "Your lean-to is similar to shelters used on hunting trips. It's different from his house in the village."

"What did Red Bird say when he pointed at us?" asked Simon.

"He doesn't understand why you and Nicolas quarrel. His people, even the children, seldom argue." Simon glanced at Nicolas and shrugged. The commandant added, "Families in his village are fun-loving, so he likes the way you boys tease." He paused and said to Nicolas. "He hopes you will live with them."

"Me?" Nicolas felt his face grow hot.

André had listened to the conversation. He said, "Red Bird may call you 'Nicolas *Humma*' when he hears that you saved Simon's life. '*Humma*' added to a man's name gives him distinction, calling forth courage and honor." Speaking in the Mobilian jargon, André told Red Bird about Simon's accident. The look on Red Bird's face left no doubt that he was impressed.

"I'm not brave," said Nicolas, visualizing the experience of hiding in the bushes. He imagined from the commandant's expression that he was also thinking about it.

"*Au contraire,*" said the commandant. "I'm glad to hear of your heroism. True bravery is doing what needs to be done at the time. I've done things in battle that were considered brave. At the time I was terrified—but I did it anyway."

Nicolas nodded that he understood.

"Other times I made the wrong choice. No one is perfect, but there's a difference between bravery and foolishness," said the commandant. "Learn from mistakes; don't let them defeat you."

Nicolas looked into his eyes and gave another slight nod.

Commandant Bienville spoke to Red Bird. The boy looked at Nicolas and smiled as he responded. The commandant said, "I asked if he had to go back to the mainland today. He does, because the families are leaving for their village."

"Where is it?" asked Simon.

"It's up the Mobile River." The commandant looked at Nicolas. "I also asked if he wanted me to bring you when I come. You saw his response. Do you want to go?"

Nicolas was so surprised that he said hesitantly, *"Mais oui.* Is my father going?"

"Non, he's too busy to leave right now. He'll come up later."

Nicolas wanted to go, but he remembered Claude's wicked laugh. What if the commandant decides to leave me in the village, he thought, even if I don't want to stay? His expression revealed his indecision.

"Tell your father I said you're going with us." Commandant Bienville's words sounded like an order. Nicolas felt stunned. He barely heard the good-byes to Red Bird. "Walk him to his canoe," the commandant said to Nicolas. "I told him you'll see him in about five days."

Simon asked, "What about me? Can I go?"

He put his hand on Simon's shoulder. "Your mother needs you here to protect her and François when your father joins us in a couple of weeks."

Simon frowned and said firmly, "I can't protect anybody. I want to go so you can protect me!"

The commandant chuckled. "Not this time."

Nicolas, anxious about the trip, couldn't think of anything to say to Red Bird. Fortunately, Simon talked nonstop all the way to the canoe. Nicolas pointed to the sun and held up five fingers. Red Bird nodded that he understood. He pushed the canoe into the water, turned it toward the shore of the mainland, and paddled away.

Nicolas sensed that something important was about to happen, but he had no idea what it was. His fear had turned to excitement by the time they got to the camp. He dashed up to his parents, who were sitting near the fire, and breathlessly spilled out the commandant's message.

"It's too dangerous to go without your father," said his mother.

"Of course, he'll go," said his father. "If the commandant invited him, he can't refuse." He gave Nicolas a firm pat on the back. "This is just what you need."

The next few days passed quickly as Nicolas, Simon, and their mother worked on the new shelter. Their father stayed busy at the supply tents, impatiently waiting while Antoine Le Moyne directed the construction of the warehouse.

Late in the afternoon of January 10—five days after their arrival on the island—Nicolas and Simon came upon Commandant Bienville talking to their father. The commandant said to Nicolas, "We'll leave in the morning to go upriver. When a decision is made about the location of the settlement, you can help clear under-brush."

"*Oui,* monsieur." Nicolas glanced at his father and asked, "When will you come?"

When his father answered, "In about a week," Nicolas frowned.

Half-teasing, the commandant said, "I think he's afraid I'm going to leave him with the Mobilians." Nicolas wondered if he could read his thoughts. In a serious voice the commandant said to him, "I'll take good care of you."

"Of course, you will," said Monsieur La Salle. He looked at Nicolas and leaned his head toward Commandant Bienville. "You can learn valuable lessons from him."

Nicolas remembered the promise he'd made to himself to watch and listen. He hadn't realized it would mean this. The commandant waited for his reaction, so Nicolas said in a strong voice, "Monsieur, I want to learn all I can. I'm sorry I didn't thank you for inviting me to go to Red Bird's village."

"I understand," said the commandant holding a steady gaze on Nicolas. Finally he glanced at the unfinished warehouse and said to Monsieur La Salle, "I'm leaving ten men with Antoine to finish the roof." Turning back to Nicolas, he said, "I'll see you at the landing in the morning." He smiled and added, "You won't be the same boy when you return."

I wonder what he meant by that, thought Nicolas. His hand went to his stomach, which was making all kinds of strange noises. His eyes followed the commandant as he moved among the workers, laughing and joking.

His father said, "This is quite an opportunity. When Commandant Bienville chooses the site for the capital of La Louisiane, you'll be there!"

Nicolas tried to smile, but his face felt stiff. He rubbed his churning stomach.

Simon gave him a questioning look. "If you decide to stay here, I'll take your place. It's not fair that I can't go."

"Simon! I'm going!"

Early the next morning, Monsieur La Salle checked off supplies as sailors loaded two feluccas, small narrow sailing ships. Captain Joseph Le Moyne watched another man check off items being loaded into the launch, the medium-sized three-masted boat he was sailing. Nicolas helped carry sickles, axes, and others tools onto one of the feluccas. When it was loaded, Commandant Bienville, Monsieur Charles Levasseur (carrying a small portable desk), Père Dongé, André, Claude and his dog, Nicolas, and several workers boarded the felucca. Sailors got into place to row the ship away from shore and, whenever the wind slackened too much, to use sails. Claude sat in the bow of the small ship and looked straight ahead as he scratched his dog's head.

Monsieur Levasseur, a Canadian lieutenant who often laughed and joked, sat next to Nicolas. He was about the age of Nicolas's father and had also explored with Robert Cavelier de La Salle. As the felucca sailed up the bay, Monsieur Levasseur opened his portable desk, which was filled with art supplies. Nicolas watched him sketch canes in thick patches along the shore and tall dead grass in the marshes. Farther up the bay, he drew pine trees and large oaks on the bluffs.

"Have you been to the Mobilian villages before?"

asked Nicolas.

"*Mais oui.* A couple of years ago, several of us Canadians explored the Mobile-Alabama River and its branches. We visited the villages then."

"So they're friendly?"

"*Bien sûr!* Without their help, and especially the corn they gave us, we might have starved at Fort Maurepas. Some of the Canadian men even lived in the Mobilian villages for awhile when food was scarce at the fort."

"Are there a lot of tribes along the rivers?"

Monsieur Levasseur nodded. "A man from another tribe, living with the Mobilians, gave me the names of 36 small nations. They live along the Mobile-Alabama River—from the Mobilian villages north to the place where two rivers come together in the land of the Alabama tribe."

When Nicolas saw a frown darken the lieutenant's usually smiling face, he asked, "What's wrong?"

"This Indian man said that English traders come into these nations and bring packhorses loaded with guns, powder, and things to trade for buckskins and buffalo hides," said Monsieur Levasseur. "But they also trade guns for women and children."

"You mean slaves?" asked Nicolas, shocked.

"*Mais oui.* Tribes war with their neighbors, killing the men and enslaving the women and children. It's caused terrible destruction among the Pensacola Indians and Mobilians."

Nicolas shook his head. That's why I don't want to live in a village, he thought. "How many Mobilians are there?"

"When I was here a couple of years ago, there were five villages, with about five hundred people, including women and children. But I doubt there are that many now."

"Why?"

"Raids on their villages and disease. Unfortunately, Native people have caught diseases from us, and many have died," said Monsieur Levasseur.

In the late afternoon, the ships stopped for the night at the mouth of a small river on the western shore of Mobile Bay. Nicolas, anxious to stretch his legs, was one of the first off the ship. Claude and his dog were last.

Nicolas watched him throw a stick for Chienne to fetch. When Claude tired, he sat down and leaned against a tree. The dog laid her head on his feet. At least Chienne loves him, thought Nicolas. No one else wants to be around him, especially me.

The thought had barely flashed through his mind before Commandant Bienville called, "Claude, you and Nicolas gather firewood."

Not again, thought Nicolas. Dread covered him like storm clouds over the bay.

Claude pointed his finger at Nicolas. "Can the wilting lily pick up a few sticks?" A mocking grin seemed permanently glued on his face. *"Mais oui!* A wilting lily!"

Nicolas's ears burned. He thought, I'm going to wilt that grin on your face! Heading away from Claude, he gathered an armload of sticks. When he brought them to the shore,

102

he heard Chienne barking in the distance.

A few minutes later, he was searching the ground for larger pieces of wood when he heard the dog barking again. He stood and looked down the riverbank. Claude was gathering wood near the trees. Chienne was at the edge of the water barking furiously. Nicolas saw a large piece of tree bark floating on the water. I guess she wants to fetch sticks again, he thought.

Claude whistled, and Chienne moved back a few steps but continued to bark. He whistled again and walked toward the dog.

What Nicolas had believed to be tree bark was actually the head of an alligator! It rose to the surface and glided silently through the water. Chienne barked even louder as the alligator came ashore. Suddenly, it moved with incredible speed, and the dog turned to flee. Nicolas, frozen in terror, watched the gigantic jaws open. In a flash, they closed around Chienne's neck—so quickly she didn't make a sound. The alligator rolled over and over in the water, taking Chienne with it. Claude let out a blood-curdling shriek and ran toward the river. By the time he reached the water, there was no alligator and no Chienne.

Nicolas's heart was racing so fast he thought it would burst. He dropped the wood, hid behind a tree, and covered his ears, trying to block out Claude's pitiful cries for Chienne. When the cries turned into sobs, Nicolas peeked around the tree. The boy sat at the edge of the water, head resting on his drawn-up knees and covered with his folded arms. Nicolas realized that Claude didn't know he

he was near. He eased into the forest and made his way back to the beach, picking up pieces of wood as he went.

When he got back, André took one look at him and asked, "What happened to you? Did you see a ghost?"

Nicolas told how the alligator had attacked the dog. He thought, No need to tell everything. So he only said, "Claude is very upset."

André shook his head sadly. "Another *Rivière aux Chien.*"

"What do you mean?" asked Nicolas.

"When we were exploring a river east of the mouth of the Mississippi, an alligator ate a man's dog. So we named the river, *Rivière aux Chien*—Dog River."

No telling how Claude will act after this, thought Nicolas. He dreaded seeing the boy again.

CLAUDE'S CONFESSION

It was nearly dark when Claude, his shoulders hunched and eyes downcast, trudged back to the beach with an armload of wood. Word of his misfortune had spread, so the usual laughing and joking stopped when he approached the men gathered around the fire. Claude cautiously glanced around. Commandant Bienville stepped forward and put his hand on the boy's shoulder. "We're sorry about your dog."

"How'd you find out so fast?" he asked, taking a step back so that the commandant's hand fell away.

Commandant Bienville frowned slightly but said in a kind voice, "Nicolas told us." Claude scowled at Nicolas as the commandant continued. "Several of our men witnessed something similar a while back. It's terrible, especially when it's your pet."

Claude grunted. "It was just a dog!" He whirled around, snatched up his bedroll, and stomped off. Later when Nicolas and the others had finished eating, they saw Claude leaning against the tree he'd sat under earlier with Chienne. The men gave each other questioning looks. Then they moved off to prepare for the night. Claude slept at the foot of the tree.

The next morning, he did his chores with a bad-tempered expression and only spoke when asked a direct question. He was first on the boat and went to the exact spot where he had sat the day before.

Nicolas sat beside Père Dongé. From time to time, he glanced at Claude, but the boy stared straight ahead as the boat sailed north up the bay. Once the priest tried to talk with him, but Claude refused to speak.

About midmorning, Nicolas's mouth dropped open and he exclaimed, "Look at that!" He tapped Père Dongé's shoulder and pointed to a large cross on a bluff overlooking Mobile Bay.

"I wonder how that got there," said the priest.

Monsieur Levasseur, sitting nearby, smiled and said, "I'm glad you like it! I put it there."

"When?" asked Nicolas, thinking he was joking.

"A couple of years ago. Yesterday I told you about my visit to the Mobilian villages. In the first one, I saw a large cross. When I asked about it, the Indians said that the Spanish had put it there. They also gave them two hogs—no doubt to win their friendship." He pointed northeast across the bay. "The Pensacola tribe lived over there then. I spent the night with them after leaving the Mobilians. The next day I crossed this bay, which the Spanish named Bay of the Holy Spirit. I decided since the Spanish were planting crosses in the Indian villages, I'd build an eight-foot cross to let them know that the land on this side of the bay belongs to France."

Père Dongé shook his head and said softly, "That's not what the cross is for."

The lieutenant's face colored slightly, and he looked down at his hands. "You are right. Land and riches can become more important than people."

"That's why Indians around here don't trust white men, especially the Spanish," said Père Dongé. "You know what Hernando de Soto did to them."

"What?" asked Nicolas.

"Several hundred Spanish men wearing suits of armor and carrying guns came through the land on horses. The Indians had never seen anything like it. The men stole the Indians' food and killed or enslaved many of them." Père Dongé sighed. "It's been almost two hundred years, but stories are still passed down about the cruel white men that rode 'big deer.'"

"They almost wiped out Chief Tuskaloosa's tribe in a battle at Mauvilla," said Monsieur Levasseur with deep sadness in his voice. "It was one of the largest tribes in this region at the time."

Père Dongé asked, "Don't some people believe the Mobilians descended from the people of that tribe?" Monsieur Levasseur nodded.

"How did you find out about this?" asked Nicolas.

"Père Du Ru told me," said the priest.

"Some of Hernando de Soto's men kept journals," said Monsieur Levasseur. "When they got back to Spain, news spread."

André soon joined them, and the men continued their conversation. Nicolas grew bored, so he lay down and took a nap. When he woke up, Claude was still sitting in the bow of the boat all alone. Feeling sorry for him, Nicolas decided to risk speaking to him. He edged along the side of the ship until he was beside him. Then he glanced at him and said, "The wind is much colder here than where I was sitting."

Claude didn't look at him. He pulled his coat tighter.

Nicolas braced himself for insults as he said, "I'm really sorry about Chienne." He quickly added, "I only told André how the alligator attacked. I just said you were upset."

Claude scowled and asked, "That's all?" When Nicolas nodded, he said suspiciously, "You didn't tell him anything else about me?"

"*Non!* I said, 'Claude is very upset.' Those were my exact words."

The red-haired boy looked relieved for a moment, but then his stony face returned.

"We had an old dog in Toulon," said Nicolas, facing Claude as he leaned against the ship's railing. Remembering his pet, Nicolas could almost feel the rough tongue licking his hand as he buried his face in the thick brown fur. "She was plain, but we loved her." After a moment he asked, "Did you have a dog when you were at home?"

Claude nodded but continued to stare straight ahead. When Nicolas had almost given up on him answering,

Claude said gruffly, "I had a little dog once."

"What kind was it?" asked Nicolas.

"She looked a lot like Chienne," said Claude with a catch in his voice. "I never should have let anyone know about her."

"Why not?"

Claude's whole body seemed to shrink, and he ducked his head as if the memory were a physical blow. "Because everything I love, dies!" A lone tear slipped out of the corner of his eye. He swiped it away, squared his shoulders, and stared into the distance.

"What happened?" asked Nicolas, quietly.

"My older brother was mad with me, so he kicked her in the head, and she died. So there! Are you satisfied?"

Nicolas lowered his head, eased down beside Claude, and listened to the wind in the sails.

Finally Claude said in a low voice, "I didn't steal anything."

"Huh?" Nicolas didn't know what to say.

"I didn't steal anything from those trunks or from my brother." Claude's eyes challenged him. "If I tell you something, don't laugh."

"I promise!" He was too scared to laugh at Claude, anyway.

"You won't believe it, and you'll use it against me."

Looking straight into his eyes without flinching, Nicolas said, "Non, I won't!"

"The reason I look in trunks is to find out what's special to the person. It's usually something very small—like a locket with the hair of the sailor's sweetheart in it, or something that belonged to his mother." Claude shrugged. "It's like I know something about the real person, not just the tough side everybody sees on the ship."

Nicolas said, hesitantly, "I think I understand."

After a long pause, Claude smiled slyly. "I use such information from time to time . . . when I'm desperate."

Nicolas's eyes widened. "You threaten to embarrass the sailor by telling everybody if he doesn't do what you want?"

"I need something for protection. Even the meanest sailor has a soft spot, and I want to know what it is."

Shaking his head in disapproval, Nicolas said, "There are other ways."

"Well, I haven't found them!" Claude said, "My jealous brother makes everybody believe I stole my mother's diamond ring from him, but I didn't. That's why he sent me off as a cabin boy." He stared into the distance for a while before he said, "She gave me the ring before she died. Maman knew that as the oldest son, my brother would get all the inheritance, and she wanted me to have something."

Nicolas studied Claude for a long time. "I believe you," he said finally. "But it's better to find ways to help people, instead of using things against them."

"That's easy for you to say," said Claude. After a pause, he said, "Maybe you could put in a good word for me with your father and Commandant Bienville."

Nicolas's mouth dropped open. "You mean, try to get them to believe that you didn't steal anything?" Claude nodded. "A word from me won't make any difference." When he looked into Claude's pleading eyes, he said, "But I'll . . . do what I can."

FEAR OF THE UNKNOWN

A strong wind kept the ships from making good time. As it got late in the afternoon, Nicolas paced the ship's deck, rubbing his hands up and down the sleeves of his *capote*. He thought, What if the Indians don't want us in their villages and try to hurt us. What will I do then? I don't know how to fight. He glanced at Monsieur Levasseur. He seemed calm—laughing and joking as usual. André also seemed relaxed.

Père Dongé joined him in his pacing. "I've been watching you, and I feel the way you look. Doing something new is scary, isn't it?" Nicolas nodded. The priest gestured toward André and Monsieur Levasseur and said, "They've been here before, so they know what to expect. Since they seem at ease, why don't we follow their example and relax?"

"*Oui,* monsieur. Red Bird wanted me to come, so I'm sure everything will be all right," said Nicolas. But his voice sounded doubtful.

Just before sunset, Nicolas spotted a rectangular cabin on the riverbank. He grabbed Monsieur

Levasseur's arm and pointed toward it. "Does an Indian live there?" he asked, trying to keep his voice from trembling.

Monsieur Levasseur nodded. "Mobilian cabins are spread out on both sides of the river for about fifteen miles." He smiled kindly at Nicolas and said, "I've already told you they are friends."

Nicolas said, "I know. I know." He clutched the railing of the ship and watched more cabins go by. They had high mud-covered walls, and the palmetto fronds on the roofs were held down with split cane. We need to do that to our lean-to, so the fronds won't blow off, Nicolas thought. He turned and asked Monsieur Levasseur, "Why are the cabins so spread out? I expected them to be close together."

"Outside of the villages, they leave space between the cabins to grow their crops."

"Does the village where we're going have a name?" asked Nicolas.

Monsieur Levasseur nodded. "It's called Mauvilla, and there are about forty cabins on an island. But don't get it confused with Chief Tuskaloosa's Mauvilla. That village was farther inland.

The sun had set when the group arrived. Red Bird was at the front of the crowd that had gathered to greet them. He was dressed the same as the last time Nicolas saw him. With gestures, he let Nicolas know that it was a great honor to have him among his people. He kept making hand signals and repeating something Nicolas

116

couldn't understand.

Nicolas turned to André. "What is Red Bird saying?"

After André had talked with the Indian boy for a moment, he said, "He will spend tonight here in his uncle's hut, but tomorrow he wants to take you to his village."

"Oh, I don't know. I'll have to do whatever Commandant Bienville wants."

"Then you'll have plenty of time to go with Red Bird," said André. "The commandant has his mind on one thing, and that's the settlement's location."

"Papa wants me to be with him when he makes that decision," said Nicolas.

André shook his head. "I don't think there's much chance of that."

"Do you mean he's going to leave me here?" Nicolas's hand went to his stomach. It wasn't feeling too good. "He said he wouldn't leave me."

"He won't be gone long—maybe a day." André put his arm around Nicolas's shoulder. "Besides, I'll be here."

"Good," said Nicolas, giving a sigh of relief. He smiled at Red Bird, who was watching him closely.

The *mingo* gestured for Commandant Bienville to lead the way. He walked behind the commandant, and everyone followed. The *mingo* and several other men wore skin robes with the wool on the inside. "That's a good way to keep warm," said Nicolas. "What kind of animal skin are those robes?"

117

"Buffalo." André pointed to other robes and said, "Those are deer-skin as well as their shoes." He nodded toward a man and said, "That is bear-skin, and those women are wearing turkey-feather cloaks." Some men wore similar cloaks.

There was so much to see that Nicolas tried to look in all directions at once. When he sniffed several times, Red Bird pointed toward the roof of a house up ahead. Smoked seeped from cracks in the palmetto-frond roof. As they got closer to the houses, Nicolas saw small fires in front of most of them. The smell of smoke was comforting on this cold evening. It reminded him of Massacre Island when his family gathered around the fire to eat, and he could see small groups of men gathered around their fires. The villagers smiled shyly, and children peeped from behind their mothers. Nicolas took a deep breath and walked taller.

"When we get to the *mingo's* cabin, you will be offered food," said André. "Eat whatever the women bring, or the people will think you don't like them."

"I'm too nervous to eat."

"Eat it anyway! We don't want to hurt our friends' feelings."

Nicolas gulped. I hope I don't get sick, he thought.

The *mingo's* large cabin was soon crowded. He greeted each guest, shook hands, and pointed to beds along the wall.

When he was seated between André and Red Bird, Nicolas whispered to André, "What did he say?"

"He asked, 'Are you there, my friend?' It's like us asking, 'how are you,' or something. It's just a way to make visitors feel welcome."

Everyone was quiet as the chief greeted the rest of the visitors.

Nicolas gazed around the room in wonder. Cane beds about three feet high lined the walls. They were covered with skins of buffalo, deer, and bear and were being used now as tables and chairs instead of beds. A low fire was burning in the middle of the cabin.

After everyone was seated, there were a few minutes of silence. Finally Commandant Bienville made a short speech in a language the people evidently understood. Nicolas saw several Native people smiling and nodding.

"Was that the Mobilian language?" asked Nicolas.

"*Non,*" said André, "it was the Mobilian jargon, but you could tell they understood a lot of what he said."

"They might have understood, but I didn't!"

"He told them how happy we are to be here."

The women brought out meat, bread, stew in clay bowls, water to drink, and wooden spoons. I'm not sure I can do this, Nicolas thought, watching Red Bird enjoying the food. He pointed to the stew and asked André, "What is this?"

"Sagamite—a stew made from corn and beans." André pointed toward something hanging from the eaves of the house. "Those are dried black-eyed peas. Some of them may be in it too. It's good."

After eating a tiny bite, Nicolas said, "You're right."

He was hungrier than he had thought. He took a bite of the meat. "Ummm . . . this is good."

"It is smoked buffalo," said André. Nicolas leaned toward him. It was difficult to hear with so many talking. André spoke louder. "The bread is made from corn."

Nicolas saw two women in the corner put their hands over their mouths to keep from laughing. He nodded toward them. "What do they think is funny?"

André asked Red Bird. He smiled timidly and didn't seem to want to answer. Finally, he gave a long reply, which caused André to chuckle.

"What's going on?" asked Nicolas, feeling left out.

BURIAL CUSTOMS

"Red Bird said his people only speak one at a time," said André. "If they must talk to someone else, it's so low others can't hear them. They think it's funny when several Frenchmen talk at the same time. They say we sound like a flock of geese."

Nicolas smiled as he glanced at the women. He saw the *mingo* speak to Commandant Bienville. Then the *mingo* made a speech to the gathering. Nicolas was so tired that his head kept nodding forward and jerking back. Finally the speech ended, and the villagers began to leave. "What did he say?" Nicolas asked André.

"He said, 'Attention! Listen you to my brief remarks.' That's their usual greeting, but as you saw, it wasn't brief. He welcomed us and then explained that since it's late and the honored guests are tired, the tribal dance will be tomorrow night."

"*Bien!* Good!" said Nicolas. "I can't hold my eyes open much longer." He saw Red Bird smile when a dignified Mobilian man came over, bowed slightly, and shook hands with André. He nodded toward Nicolas and spoke several sentences.

André said, "This is Red Bird's father, *mingo* of

Totechoco, a nearby village. He is the brother of the headman here. We honor them with our presence. Red Bird told him of your kindness. He invites you to come to his village tomorrow. He says that his home is your home."

Nicolas's face felt frozen as he tried to smile. He said hesitantly, "Thank you," which André translated. Red Bird and his father said good night, and Nicolas watched them walk toward beds at the far end of the large room. He tried to breathe normally as he fought the urge to run and hide. He took a deep breath and turned toward André, "He doesn't mean *live* with them, does he?"

André shook his head and smiled sympathetically. "If I didn't remember how scared I was my first night in a Native village, I would laugh my head off right now. But lucky for you, it seems like yesterday."

"So what do we do now?" asked Nicolas, turning away to hide his embarrassment.

"Get our things and hop into one of these beds."

Nicolas looked around as he followed André to the corner where they'd left their bedrolls. Even though the villagers and many of the Frenchmen had left, there were still about a dozen Indians still in the cabin. "We're sleeping here with all these people?"

André nodded and said, "They're the family and relatives of the *mingo*."

Commandant Bienville, Captain Joseph Le Moyne, Monsieur Levasseur, and Nicolas chose beds at one end

124

of the room. André, Père Dongé, and Claude were along the side. The heads of Nicolas's and André's beds met in the corner. The *mingo's* family and relatives filled the rest of the room.

Not sure what to do, Nicolas watched André. Following his example, Nicolas spread his bedroll on the bearskin, then put a buffalo skin at the foot of his bed to use for cover. He took off his shoes and outer clothes, and climbed into his bed, covering himself with his blanket. As he thought about Maman and Papa, he felt terribly homesick, even though home was only a lean-to. He missed François and even Simon with all of his whining and complaining. If Papa knew how I've felt today, he would be ashamed of me, thought Nicolas. Père Dongé knew I was scared, and now so does André. The priest's words echoed in his mind. "I feel the way you look. Doing something new is scary, isn't it?" Nicolas gave careful thought to these words. Hmmm . . . he's a grown man, but evidently he meant he was scared too. I can understand Commandant Bienville's fear during a battle, but this is different. I've never thought about men being afraid just like boys. Even André admitted it. He said that he wouldn't laugh at me, because he remembered how scared he had been his first night in a Native village. Nicolas gave a sigh of relief. He felt better knowing that he wasn't the only one who had felt scared. As he pulled up the buffalo skin, he saw André lying on his side writing in a book. Nicolas raised up on his elbow and asked,

"What are you doing?"

"I'm writing in my journal."

"What do you write about?"

"Mostly about people and places," said André. "I'm not too concerned about dates or day-to-day activities. Who knows . . . maybe someday these notes will become a book." With a look of pride, he said, "My godfather was an author."

Commandant Bienville walked over and put his things on the bed at Nicolas's feet. "How are things going?"

"Bien, monsieur," said Nicolas. "The food is better than I expected." He glanced around the room. "Where are the other men?"

"In the cabin next door." After the commandant was in bed, he said, "I'm at your feet, and André is at your head, so sleep well. Tomorrow will be a busy day."

"Oui, monsieur." Nicolas yawned and snuggled under the warm covers. Maybe that means I'm going with him, he thought.

Awaking with a start, Nicolas couldn't remember where he was. The smell of smoke filled the room, and he felt as if he couldn't breathe. His heart thumped wildly as he heard a noise near his bed. He peeked through half-closed eyes. When he saw Commandant Bienville in the early morning light, he sat up.

"Pardon," said the commandant softly. "The end of

my bed bumped against yours when I got up."

Nicolas nodded sleepily and turned on his side with his back to the wall. A few minutes later, he opened his eyes and saw the commandant changing his shirt. He was surprised to see his chest tattooed with figures of snakes.

The commandant must have felt him staring, because he looked down at Nicolas. He proudly patted his chest and whispered, "My Mobilian friends did this. Their warriors have tattoos of snakes, and when I go to war with them, I want to be as much like them as possible." He turned and finished dressing.

Nicolas's heart beat faster as he thought, War? There's going to be a war?

When the commandant turned around, Nicolas whispered urgently, "When is there going to be a war?"

"Don't worry," whispered the commandant with a reassuring smile. "The Indians are constantly fighting each other— just like the French are always fighting the English or Spanish." He sighed heavily. "But my job is to try to bring peace." He looked earnestly at Nicolas and leaned closer. "And you can help."

"Me!" said Nicolas.

"You're Red Bird's friend, aren't you?" When Nicolas nodded, the commandant said, "Well, friends help bring peace."

Nicolas lay back on his bed and stared at the embers of the fire in the middle of the cabin. I guess that's why Governor Iberville is helping the Spanish at Pensacola, and they are helping us.

Soon others began to stir. Monsieur Levasseur and Captain Joseph dressed quietly. Nicolas again sat up in bed, trying to decide if he should also get dressed. The commandant bent down to him and pointed to the two men as he said in a low voice, "The three of us and Red Bird's father are going downstream to choose the settlement's location. Claude is staying with Père Dongé so an old man in the village can teach them some basic Mobilian words. André will go with you to Red Bird's village, so do whatever he says."

Nicolas said, "But . . . . "

The commandant held up his hand to stop further comments. Then he turned quickly and left with the men.

Red Bird, eager to be on the way right after breakfast, motioned for André to lead as the three started through the village. When they got to the riverbank, Red Bird led them to a dugout canoe. It only took a few minutes to paddle across the river from the island to the western bank. Nicolas glanced at the cabins along the riverbank as they headed inland. He inhaled the pine-scented air as they walked single file on a path through the woods. He felt safe with André ahead and Red Bird behind him. The bright, clear day wasn't as cold as the past few days had been, and the rays of sunlight filtering through the tree branches warmed his face. As he listened to birds chirping and small animals scurrying through the brush, Nicolas felt a new sense of contentment. He was disappointed that he couldn't go with Commandant Bienville. But, after eating with the villagers and spending the night in the *mingo's* cabin, he didn't feel as nervous about being around Native people. He would rather have stayed at Mauvilla for the day, but Nicolas knew Red Bird wanted to show him his village.

He heard a noise in the distance. He strained his ears, trying to identify the high-pitched sound. He glanced back at Red Bird, but the boy seemed to be avoiding eye contact. "What's that noise?" he whispered to André.

"We're near a cabin," he answered, with an uneasy tone in his voice.

Nicolas tensed. What's going on, he wondered. He wrinkled his nose as he got a whiff of a terrible odor. "Phew! There's something dead around here."

André looked back at him, and from the slight shake of his head, Nicolas knew it was a signal to be quiet. As they came around a curve in the path, he spotted the cabin. A short distance in front of it, two women wailed as they trudged around a raised platform with a coffin-shaped cabin on it. The older woman had her arm around the younger, trying to keep her from collapsing.

André stepped behind him and whispered to Red Bird. Nicolas's pulse raced as he stared at the platform. "What's wrong?" he asked.

André took the lead again and said, "A boy about eight years old died a few days ago. His mother and grand-mother come each day to mourn as they circle the scaffold."

Nicolas felt the blood drain from his face. By this

time, they were almost to the cabin. André nodded respectfully to the women, so Nicolas did the same.

After they had walked a little way, Nicolas whispered to the back of André's head, "When will they bury him?"

"They won't. He'll stay up there several months."

"What?" Shaking his head hard, he tried to grasp what he'd just heard, but his brain had shut down. He was dizzy, and he kept swallowing hard to keep from throwing up. He prayed silently, "God, please don't let me get sick where those poor women can see me!" He glimpsed the next cabin through the trees. We'll soon be away from the smell, he told himself. He concentrated on the cabin ahead and willed himself to get out of sight of the women and make it past the next cabin.

Eight years old—the same age as Simon, he thought. He remembered the dead weight on him in the boat and the tears in his mother's eyes when she said, "I don't know what I'd have done if . . . ." Maman could be mourning for Simon just like those women. Nicolas gagged and ran into the bushes. When there was nothing left to throw up, he sank into the weeds and sobbed brokenheartedly.

André put a firm hand on Nicolas's back. "The first time is tough. I'll have to tell you my experience someday." He spoke to Red Bird, who was standing to the side, waiting patiently. Then he said, "I told him you are sad because the boy was the same age as your brother." Nicolas nodded. André helped him to his feet.

"It is important to show respect for this tribe's burial customs. They are different from our French customs, but that doesn't make them wrong."

Nicolas was almost too weak to walk. However, Red Bird proudly introduced Nicolas and André to everybody they saw as they made their way into the small village. Red Bird's house was the largest in Totechoco but not as big as the *mingo's* house in Mauvilla. His mother, a small, thin woman with a blanket around her, welcomed them into the house and invited them to sit on a bed. His younger brothers and sister gazed at them with curiosity as they all sat a few minutes in silence, as they had done last night at the *mingo's* house.

André spoke in their language, and then translated it for Nicolas. He said it was an honor to be in their home and to be welcomed into the village. Red Bird's mother smiled warmly as she asked him to tell Nicolas how pleased she was to meet him. Red Bird had told her many good things about him. She excused herself to get them something to eat.

She served cooked pumpkin, water, and bread cakes made from corn. Nicolas drank the water, but he didn't think he could eat anything. Then he remembered what André had said about Native food customs, so he took a little bite of pumpkin. "Mmm . . . delicious," he said, licking the wooden spoon. He was glad to get rid of that vomit taste, and the pumpkin was really good.

"Fresh pumpkin cooked without water is almost as sweet as syrup," said André. "It's my favorite Native food." He looked around the house as he said, "I imagine these were dried pumpkins, even though I don't see any hanging anywhere."

Red Bird talked to his mother as they ate. She looked at Nicolas with pity and made comforting sounds as if he were a baby.

When Nicolas looked to André for a translation, he said, "He told her about Simon's accident and how upset you were over the little boy."

Nicolas blushed. I'll probably never live that down, he thought.

André thanked Red Bird's mother for the food. Nicolas smiled and mumbled, "Thank you." Then Red Bird led them outside. Two elderly men were sitting against the trunk of a large tree, so the group walked over to them. Red Bird lowered his head, bowed slightly, and introduced his visitors. He gestured toward Nicolas as he talked.

Nicolas figured he was telling them the same story, since they nodded sympathetically. As he hung his head in embarrassment, he glimpsed the fingernails of the man nearest him. His eyes widened as he looked again. The thumb, forefinger and middle finger of each hand had the longest nails Nicolas had ever seen. Red Bird had the men's complete attention, so Nicolas stole a quick glance at the other man's fingers. He almost gasped. His nails were even longer. He wanted to stare, but he forced himself to look up. He tried to get André's attention, but he was also listening to Red Bird.

The boy leaned his head toward André, indicating that he wanted a translation for Nicolas.

André cleared his throat and said to Nicolas, "I'll explain who they are later. I don't think you're up to it right now."

Nicolas frowned. "Why not?"

"You'll see."

THE BONE-PICKERS

Red Bird came out of the cabin carrying a racquet in each hand. He smiled as he raised them above his head, shook them, and said, *"Ishtaboli!"* As he talked to André, he pointed with a racquet to villagers gathering in a large field with goal posts at each end.

"Now I know why he wanted to get here early," said André, smiling. "He wants us to watch him play *ishtaboli*—ball-play or stickball. They're practicing for a game with another village."

Nicolas pointed to a racquet and then to himself. When Red Bird handed it to him, he examined the two-foot-long stick. One end was bent and fastened to the stick with strings of hide to form a loop. A string net was in this end.

"Raccoon skin strings," said André, when Nicolas fingered the net. "The other string is deer hide."

Glancing at the other racquet, Nicolas asked, "Is he bringing an extra one?"

"Non," said André. "Each player has two."

"So how do they play the game?" asked Nicolas, gazing

at the goals made from two tall poles with another across the top.

"The players hold a racquet in each hand, and when the medicine man throws a small deerskin ball into the air, they try to catch the ball between the two little nets. Then they throw it and try to get it between the goal posts without touching the ball with their hands."

"And that scores a point?"

André nodded and said, "In a big game, they might play until a team gets a hundred points, but usually it's sixteen."

As they approached the field, Red Bird waved good-bye and ran toward his friends. His brothers and sister had already joined theirs.

Nicolas and André sat with Red Bird's mother. Nicolas couldn't understand the conversation between the two, but Red Bird's mother smiled proudly. André turned to Nicolas and said, "The men practice with each other and then play teams from nearby villages so they can be victorious at the Green Corn Ceremony." He smiled and said, "Just like a mother, she thinks Red Bird is one of the best players."

"What is the Green Corn Ceremony?"

"About July, when the corn is ripe, they have an eight-day celebration to give thanks for good crops and settle disputes. It's the beginning of a new year."

Cheers erupted as two teams with ten players apiece lined up facing each other. "When they play another village, these twenty players make up a team. But the number of players varies with as many as six or seven hundred in some Choctaw games," said André. He nodded knowingly and said, "You'll soon see why this game is sometimes called 'Little Brother of War.'"

An old man came into the center of the field and threw a ball high into the air. Players darted around hooting and hollering as they tried to score. Those watching on the sidelines joined in with cheers and jeers.

Nicolas tried to keep Red Bird in sight as he dashed around the field. He saw him catch the ball in his racquet. Red Bird was in a good position to throw it between the goal posts when he was knocked off his feet from behind and three members from the other team pounced on him. When Red Bird's mother and others jumped to their feet, Nicolas and André did too. Spectators screamed, *"Hokli! Hokli!"*

André looked at Nicolas and shouted, *"Hokli! Hokli!* Catch! Catch!"

Nicolas tried to yell the words, not caring if they came out right or wrong. "Catch! Catch!" he yelled, jumping up and down. The other team got the ball and scored before Red Bird was back in action. The teams rested a minute after the point was scored.

When the medicine man tossed the ball up, Red Bird immediately leaped into the air and caught it. He threw it to another player, who dashed down the field as Red Bird, dodging players and racquets, headed for the goal posts. The spectators yelled, *"Falamochi! Falamochi!"*

André shouted, "Throw it back! Throw it back!"

Nicolas chanted, "Throw it back! Throw it back!" The player threw the ball to Red Bird, who hurled it between the goal posts. Loud cheers exploded around them.

The players hardly had time to catch their breath before the rest time was over. When the ball was thrown into the air again, an opponent hit Red Bird in the back with his fist and knocked him out of the way. A young man on Red Bird's team then hit that player. Before Red Bird had regained his balance, another opponent was wrestling him to the ground. The spectators yelled and hissed. Nicolas shook his fist and shouted, "You can't do that!" He grabbed André's arm. "That's not fair, is it?"

André grinned. "Anything goes in this game, except hitting with the racquet!"

Shrill cries, yelps, and barks filled the air as players tripped, dodged, and wrestled. The ball hit the ground, and in a rush to swoop it up, bodies tangled in a mass with arms, legs, and racquets sticking out in all directions. Nicolas put his hands on his hot cheeks. "I've never seen anything like this!" Several players staggered out of the heap with bloody noses. Others with bloody shins limped off the field.

"See why it's called 'Little Brother of War'?" asked André.

Nicolas nodded as Red Bird slipped past two opponents and scored. Nicolas jumped up and down and yelled louder than anybody around. He flopped on the

ground during the rest time. "I'm surprised they don't kill each other!"

"It's not unusual to have broken bones," said André. He looked solemn as he added, "Now and then, a player does get killed."

Red Bird's mother, standing with a woman and talking excitedly, pointed toward a player on the opposing team. Nicolas smiled and said to André, "Red Bird's mother takes this game seriously."

"*Mais oui!* Often the women play after the men's game. If their husbands lose, sometimes the wives get together and play to try to make up for the loss. They are skilled players—running swiftly, pushing and shoving like the men."

"Do all tribes let women play?"

"*Non.* Not many."

Red Bird's mother looked down at them and spoke to André. She pointed down the side of the field to a young woman with a baby. "She's going to get the baby and give the mother a rest," André said.

As Nicolas's eyes followed her, he saw the two elderly men with the long fingernails. He pointed toward them with his chin and asked, "Did you see their fingernails?" André nodded. A shiver ran down Nicolas's spine. "Who are they?"

André frowned and said, "I'm not sure you want to know."

"*Mais oui!*" said Nicolas, sharply. "I do! Why are you being so mysterious?"

André hesitated. "Sometimes it's best to learn things a little at a time."

"What do you mean?"

"When you're in a new place with people you don't know and ways you don't understand, it can be over-powering."

"I'm not a *bébé!*" said Nicolas. "You can tell me any-thing!"

André shrugged and said slowly, "They're called *Na foni aiowa,* bone-pickers, or actually, bone-gatherers."

Nicolas furrowed his brow. "Why?"

André sighed loudly and stared at his hands. Finally he said, "This nation of Native people don't bury their dead, as I told you about the little boy. They dress the body, put it on a platform like the one you saw, and cover it with a buffalo skin or deerskin. Then they put food, drink, and a change of clothes near the body." André's eyes were gentle as he looked into Nicolas's eyes and said, "They probably killed the little boy's pet dog and put it and his blowgun beside him. He'll have everything he needs for his journey to the next life."

Nicolas tried not to react, but his face got hot, and he knew it was turning red. He turned and stared with blind eyes at the players on the field.

"After several months, the bone-pickers come," continued André. "You can tell from the way Red Bird treated the men that they are highly respected."

"What do they do?" asked Nicolas, dreading the answer.

"They scrape the remaining flesh off the bones with

their fingernails, while the family and friends weep and mourn."

Picturing the long fingernails made his stomach churn, but Nicolas asked, "What do they do with the flesh?"

"They bury it, throw it in a field, or burn it, depending on the particular village."

While Nicolas thought about this, he glanced once more at the two old men. "What do they do with the bones?"

"The bone-picker cleans them, paints the skull red, and puts the bones in a cane basket or chest."

Nicolas had a quizzical expression as he asked, "Where do they get red paint?"

"They grind red ocher, which is iron ore, and mix it with bear fat."

Red Bird's mother was returning with the baby, so Nicolas asked anxiously, "Then what do they do with the bones?"

"The family and friends have a feast as if the person is just asleep. Afterward they mourn as they walk to the bone-house carrying the basket of bones and things from the platform." He added, "I'll show you their bone-house on our way back to Mauvilla."

As Red Bird's mother sat down, Nicolas looked at the baby strapped in a cradleboard. He made funny sounds at the baby to take his mind off what he'd just heard. Examining the board bound tightly with leather strips against the baby's head, he asked André, "Why is his head clamped down like that?"

"It's a custom of this tribe to make babies' heads flat. I don't know if they think it's handsome, or if it's a way of showing importance, or what."

Red Bird's team won the game. When he came off the field, Nicolas jumped up and pointed to the racquets. He said excitedly, "You're a good player!" André translated the message, and Red Bird smiled shyly.

He led them back to his house. Telling André that he was hungry after playing so hard, he got out the leftover pumpkin and bread.

As Red Bird brought them water, Nicolas asked André, "Isn't he going to wait for his family to eat?"

"*Non.* There's no set time for meals," said André. "They just eat whenever they get hungry. I've rarely seen Native people eating together, except at a feast like last night."

After they ate, André sat in the warm sun and wrote in his journal. Red Bird got his blowgun, made from a long cane, and some darts about the length from Nicolas's wrist to his elbow. He handed Nicolas several of them. Made from lightweight wood, each dart had a barbed stone on one end and thistledown on the other. Red Bird and Nicolas walked to the edge of the village. They passed several young boys using clumps of Spanish moss on the ground as targets for their blowguns. Nicolas, surprised by their accuracy, clapped and said, *"Bien!"*

Red Bird pointed to the boys and then to a bird flying

overhead and a squirrel chattering in a tree. He pretended to use his blowgun. Nicolas nodded that he understood.

They came to some tall bushes, and Red Bird held up his hand for Nicolas to stand still. A few moments later, when a bird landed on a nearby bush, Red Bird aimed and blew into the long cane. The bird fell on the ground, fluttered a few times, and died. Red Bird handed Nicolas the blowgun and went to pick up the dead bird. Nicolas couldn't believe his good fortune when Red Bird returned and gestured that Nicolas should learn to use the blowgun. He was eager to try. Red Bird was a patient teacher, and after some practice, Nicolas got fairly good at hitting a clump of Spanish moss. Red Bird pointed to a plump bird almost invisible in the thick dead grass. Nicolas felt a twinge of nervousness as he raised the long blowgun and carefully took aim. When the bird fell over dead, he jerked off his *toque,* threw it in the air and shouted, "I did it!" Red Bird, with a wide grin, clapped as Nicolas had done for the boys, and surprised Nicolas by saying, *"Bien!"* With hand movements, Nicolas tried to express his appreciation to Red Bird for letting him use his blowgun. He proudly carried his bird with him. Now he understood why the dead child's parents put his blowgun beside him on the platform.

Nicolas heard yells and howls of laughter coming from the woods. When he put his hand behind his ear and shrugged, Red Bird led him toward the noise.

A TOUGH GOODBYE

Red Bird and Nicolas discovered the source of the noise. Three boys about nine years old were watching another boy standing near a hornets nest in a hollow tree. Holding a switch in each hand, he hit and poked the nest. As the hornets swarmed out and covered his body, he beat them off with the switches. Nicolas couldn't believe the boy was standing there without flinching! The feat lasted for less than a minute before the boy ran away. Two of his friends laughed loudly. The third boy, scratching vigorously, had evidently had his turn with the hornets, so he motioned for the other boys to prove their bravery. Each took a turn at the torture, but none was able to stand it for more than about half a minute. Red Bird shook his head and turned to walk out of the woods. Nicolas breathed a sigh of relief. He certainly didn't want to prove his bravery in that way. He had heard of a child in France who died from insect stings.

By the middle of the afternoon, they were ready to start back to Mauvilla. Nicolas and André had said goodbye to Red Bird's family around the fire in front of their cabin. Red Bird came out with a blowgun, arrows, and a cane knife. He spoke to André, who said to Nicolas, "He wants to give you some presents."

When Red Bird handed him the gifts, Nicolas said, *"Merci! Merci!"* He looked at André. "Tell him that I was wishing for a blowgun."

"You'll use that cane knife often, too," said André. "They're as sharp or sharper than our knives."

"Please tell Red Bird I'm honored to have him as a friend!" Red Bird smiled and nodded when André told him.

Once they were on their way, Nicolas began dreading passing the burial platform. He thought, I'm going to think of ways to get even with Claude. That should make me so angry I won't think about anything else. However, when he tried to remember Claude's insults, he only thought of the boy's grief over Chienne. Finally Nicolas recalled Claude calling him a wilting lily. As he saw the cabin up ahead, he thought, that's exactly what I feel like right now—a wilting lily. I'm shriveling up on the inside and almost ready to topple over. The women were nowhere in sight, so he again imagined a wilting lily. For some strange reason, the idea of a lily just flopping over struck Nicolas as funny. He held his breath as they passed the platform and kept his eyes on the path as he envisioned a whole bunch of lilies going plop—plop—plop. He could hear Claude's voice in his head saying, "You look 'bout as strong as a wilting lily!"

Snicker. *"Mais oui!* 'Bout as strong as a wilting lily." As they rounded the curve in the path, Nicolas let out his breath and tried to stifle a giggle but ended up coughing and sputtering.

André turned around quickly and asked, "Are you all right?"

Nicolas nodded. "I was just thinking about lilies."

"You choked thinking about lilies? That's hard to believe!"

"It's true!" Nicolas smiled, and as he walked a little taller, he said under his breath, "Thanks, Claude!"

Shortly, André pointed down a path that Nicolas hadn't noticed on their way to the village. "If you look through the trees, you can see the bone-house—a raised platform with a roof that is open on both ends. The child's bones will be placed beside the baskets that hold other relatives."

"How will relatives that live in other villages know when to come to take the bones to the bone-house?"

"The bone-pickers give messengers small bundles of split cane called *oski kauwa* to carry to all the families far and near," said André.

"What do they do with a bundle of canes?" asked Nicolas, sounding astonished as he remembered the canes he'd cut.

"The pieces are only about four inches long and the size of a broom straw," said Andre, grinning at Nicolas. "They're tied into a bundle with string. These Indians measure time by 'sleeps,' so a stick is thrown away each morning after the sleep to avoid mistakes. The last stick is thrown away on the morning of the burial day. The family and friends gather for the feast and the trip to the bone-house."

"That's a good way to keep up with the passing days," said Nicolas.

"They use bundles of sticks whenever they need to measure time until an event, such as *ishtaboli* games."

Commandant Bienville and the men returned to Mauvilla at sundown. Nicolas looked at Monsieur Levasseur's sketches of two locations. He asked the commandant, "How will you decide between them?"

"Iberville makes that decision. I've sent two men cross-country to Pensacola with sketches and notes about the sites for him."

The *mingo* had called everyone together for the dance in the evening. Big fires of burning pine logs provided light around the village plaza. Red Bird and Nicolas sat with their backs to a fire to stay warm. When Nicolas saw Claude wandering around looking lonely, he waved for him to join them. Nicolas gestured to Claude and said to Red Bird, "This is Claude."

Red Bird said, "Clod," and nodded a welcome.

"This is Red Bird," said Nicolas. He was surprised when Claude greeted him in the Mobilian Jargon. "You're doing better than I am with the language," said Nicolas.

Claude had a thin smile as he said, "I spent the day

with Père Dongé and an old man from the village. We learned about fifty of the main words. Tomorrow we'll learn some more, if you want to join us."

Nicolas nodded eagerly. He turned his attention to about twenty-five Indian men in the plaza forming a circle without holding hands. They danced to the rhythm of a drum and double fist-sized rattles. After awhile, the leader blew a whistle, and the circle broke as they danced among themselves. He blew again, and they formed the ring again with amazing exactness.

"I wonder how they make those rattles," said Nicolas.

"I asked André about that last year when we were in a village," said Claude. "They dry gourds and fill them with little pebbles." He smiled faintly as he said, "They make a mean little noise, don't they?"

Nicolas nodded. He was amazed that Claude almost sounded friendly.

"I like music," said Claude in a low voice. "I often play the flute." He added quickly, "When there's no one around."

"I'd like to hear you play," said Nicolas.

Claude studied him carefully. Finally, he said, "Maybe sometime."

"So you stayed at Fort Maurepas after Governor Iberville's last voyage?"

"*Oui,*" said Claude. "We got there in December of 1699, and he went back to France the next May. He left several of us cabin boys."

"Have you done much exploring?" asked Nicolas.

"I mostly worked around the fort," said Claude, staring at the fire. "A couple of the boys are always getting me into trouble."

Always blaming someone else, thought Nicolas.

When Nicolas got to the cabin, the commandant was sitting on his bed with a portable desk on his lap. He looked up and said, "We'll stay here until the men return from Pensacola with Iberville's instructions."

"*Bien!*" said Nicolas. "I'll have more time to learn Red Bird's language. Claude learned a lot of words today." He hesitated before he said, "I think Claude is changing."

"He'll change more," said Commandant Bienville. "When we leave, he's staying."

Nicolas drew in his breath, started to speak, but decided against it. Poor Claude, he thought. I wonder what will happen to him.

The commandant looked into Nicolas's eyes and seemed to read his mind again. "Don't worry. The old man who's teaching him will take care of him."

During the next few days, Nicolas learned many words in the Mobilian jargon. Red Bird also taught him valuable lessons about living in the wilderness. He learned to identify deer, raccoon, and rabbit tracks. When he killed a rabbit with his blowgun, Red Bird taught him how to start a fire, skin the rabbit, and cook it in the woods.

Commandant Bienville called a meeting when the

messengers returned from Pensacola on January 19th.

"I'm proud of these men! They made the trip in just two days each way. They've brought news that Governor Iberville wants the settlement at the second bluff, so we will leave at sunrise."

The men chattered among themselves about the location of the settlement and preparations for leaving.

Nicolas had mixed feelings. He was eager to get started on the new settlement, but he had made many friends in the villages. He realized that what Red Bird's father had said the first night had come true: their home had become his home. Red Bird's mother treated him like a son. As headman, Red Bird's father had welcomed him into the life of the village. Nicolas had spent hours sitting near the fire listening to the two wise *Na foni aiowa* tell stories. He now looked on their fingernails with a sense of deep respect because of the role they played in carrying on the tribe's traditions.

Père Dongé said Mass before the group left the village the next morning. They carried food and gifts from the Mobilians with them to the ships. Red Bird was going with them, but Nicolas felt as if he were leaving part of his family behind as he said goodbye to Red Bird's family.

To Nicolas's amazement, he and Claude had become good friends as they studied the Mobilian jargon. Commandant Bienville had even let Claude spend one night in Red Bird's village. Nicolas waved to Claude as

the ship moved toward the middle of the river. He looked so lonely even though he was standing by the old man on the shore. Seeing the boy swipe at his eye, Nicolas took a deep breath and slowly let it out. At least he wasn't worried about Claude's safety. The people in the village, and especially the old man, probably loved him more than anybody ever had, except his mother.

Nicolas cupped his hands around his mouth and shouted, "I know a secret! You'd better start thinking of names, and Chienne won't do!" He pointed towards Red Bird's father, who had told Nicolas that he planned to give Claude a dog. A big grin covered Claude's face as he waved goodbye.

THE MYSTERY SOLVED

On January 20, 1702, the ships sailed south down the Mobile River, finally landing near a high bluff. As Nicolas climbed the steep hill with an armload of tools, he looked at the huge trees and thick brush. At least it's winter and some of the growth is dead, he thought. Also we don't have to worry about snakes.

When the ships were unloaded, Commandant Bienville called a gathering on the bluff. He said, "Père Dongé has the honor of performing the first act of clearing the ground." The priest prayed a blessing over the land and then cut a couple of bushes to officially begin the work. The young commandant looked at the men who were waiting for his directions. "Monsieur Levasseur will supervise the clearing of brush. He'll also help Captain Joseph and me in making decisions about the construction of the fort and other buildings. Follow his instructions."

Monsieur Levasseur said to André, "I've got too much

to do, so I want you to oversee the men. Let Nicolas and Red Bird work with them." André nodded. Monsieur Levasseur told the workers, "André is my assistant in clearing the land. Please do as he says." He hurried to join the two men.

André said to the workers, "Begin clearing at the bluff. As you cut the brush and small trees, pile them into heaps in rows. When the men fell the trees, the upper branches will settle on the piles. Then they can cut the trunks into about 12-foot lengths. They'll be used to build the fort or as stakes to surround it for protection."

Nicolas and Red Bird used thick knives with hooked points and curved blades called billhooks to cut the small bushes. By nightfall, there were huge piles of brush in long rows. As Nicolas stretched his aching back, he looked over the cleared ground. He couldn't deny they had made progress, but he groaned when he looked at the woods still to be cleared. It seemed like an impossible task. However, as the days went by, Nicolas began to feel a sense of pride, knowing that he was part of the building of the new capital of La Louisiane.

When his father arrived a few days later with a crew to build Fort Louis, Nicolas was glad to see him. But he felt different than he thought he would.

That night, his father said, "I get the feeling you're not the same boy who sailed from Massacre Island a few weeks ago."

Nicolas shrugged. "I learned a little about animal tracks." He smiled and added, "I can kill a rabbit with a blowgun, skin it, and cook it in the woods."

His father patted him on the back and said, "That's a good start." He seemed to search Nicolas's face as he said, "But that's not the difference I'm talking about."

Staring into the fire, Nicolas thought back over the last couple of weeks. How was he different? I almost feel like Red Bird's family is my family. I'm not afraid of bone-pickers any more. Then he had to admit to himself that Papa was right about learning the language faster when you live with the people. (But he wasn't about to tell his father.) When he could stand the silence no longer, he said, "André keeps a journal about his adventures. I think I'll keep one too."

"I kept one when I went down the Mississippi River with Cavelier de La Salle. I even wrote a paper about it when I got back to France. I'm writing an account now about settling this new land." His father stared at the glowing coals in the campfire. He said, "After claiming the land, Cavelier de La Salle's next goal was to build a French settlement on the Gulf Coast to make sure France kept the territory." He continued to stare into the fire. Finally he said, "He was a brave, generous man and sometimes joined in talking and laughing with the men, but mostly he was a loner. He was stern, but he didn't ask us to do anything he wouldn't do. He went ahead of us through snow and bitter cold, through swamps with waist-deep mud and into hostile Native villages. We saw some horrible sights, and I still have nightmares about them."

Nicolas remembered hearing Papa scream sometimes in the middle of the night. When he would ask Maman about it the next morning, she would always say, "It was just another bad dream."

His father looked into Nicolas's eyes and said, "He didn't live to see his dream come true, but you and I will see it. He didn't fail—his time just ran out. So it was all worth it—the misery, hardships, and deaths. His dream has not faded away. The land he claimed for France is already on the map."

There was such a long silence that Nicolas thought his father was finished. Then he said, "Maybe that will make up for some of the ways I failed him." He coughed, but Nicolas heard tears in his voice.

He thought his father looked old and tired. "Papa, I'm sure you did your best, like you always tell me."

His father shook his head. "I was young and scared and made foolish mistakes." He watched an ember blaze up, before he said, "But that's the cost of growing up. Now that I'm the age he was at his death, perhaps in many ways, I've become like him—stern and unbending." After a pause, he added, "But I believe in truth and honesty." He looked at Nicolas for a long time. "I should have listened to you when you said you misunderstood Commandant Bienville about 'lots of spirit' and 'lost spirit.' I've thought about it and remembered times in my childhood when I got into trouble for just such misunderstandings. I'm sorry." His father reached out and gave him the tightest bear hug Nicolas had ever had. "Son, I'm proud of you. Don't ever doubt it."

Nicolas nodded and brushed tears from his eyes. He and his father sat in silence, watching the burning wood send up a shower of sparks as a log burst in two. Nicolas pulled his blanket tighter around him and listened to the crackle and pop of the fire. An owl hooted in the distance. Finally he said, "You were right about me learning the language faster when I'm with the people. But I was afraid of them." He looked over at Red Bird, fast asleep on the other side of the fire. "I've learned to love Red Bird, his family, and the Mobilians."

The fire had burned down to glowing coals by the time Nicolas finished telling about the bone-house. He asked, "Do the bones stay in there forever?"

"*Non,*" said his father. "When it's full, a day is set aside and all the people gather. The nearest relatives or closest friends take all the baskets of bones and personal things from the bone-house. They mourn and shout, 'Alleluia!' as they slowly make their way to the place of burial. Then the baskets are placed in order to form a pyramid. When they are covered with earth, it forms a large mound. After the mourners return to the village, they have a feast."

That night, as Nicolas lay in his bedroll, he tried to remember what he'd heard Governor Iberville say about the place of the massacre. He clearly remembered the skulls and bones, but what was it about household things? He rolled over and stared at the glowing coals. It was something about them rotting. He turned so much that his blanket got twisted. Finally as he sat up to straighten his blanket, he remembered that they hadn't rotted. But what was it that hadn't rotted?

Nicolas found André the next morning and said, "I couldn't sleep last night for thinking about Massacre Island."

"I guess you're looking forward to seeing your mother."

"Non," said Nicolas, "I mean *oui!* But that's not what kept me awake. I overheard Governor Iberville telling Papa when we were on the *Renommée* how Massacre Island got its name. I was wondering if you've seen the pile of bones?"

André nodded. "Governor Iberville, Bienville, and Ensign Sauvole—later the commandant of Fort Maurepas—found them in February of 1699. They told us about them. After Governor Iberville left for France in May, some of us from Fort Maurepas sailed with Commandant Bienville east along the coast. We came to the island and went ashore. We were terrified when we saw the mountain of bones."

Nicolas's eyes got wide. "It was a *mountain?*"

André looked a little sheepish. "Maybe mound would be a better word."

"Were they just piled on top of each other?"

"*Oui* and *non.* The mound was covered with earth, but some of the skulls and bones were partly uncovered. When we raked off the earth, we found piles of bones."

"What about household things like bowls and cane baskets?" asked Nicolas.

"*Oui,* I think we found some. Why?"

Nicolas told what his father had said about the burial when the bone-house is full.

André scratched his chin. "At the time, we knew very little about Native customs. Governor Iberville said it was a massacre, so we didn't question it. I've never thought about it, but I see what you mean. Most likely it *was* a burial mound. A storm probably destroyed part of it, exposing the bones and skulls."

Nicolas rubbed his hands together and asked breathlessly, "Will you show me the place when we get back to the island?"

"I can't. Governor Iberville wants the ships' carpenters to build a small ship as soon as we get back."

"Why does he need another ship?" asked Nicolas, kicking a rock with the toe of his shoe.

"He wants a flat-bottomed sailboat that can be used in shallow river waters as well as in the Gulf," said André. "Besides, the mound is easy to find."

Work on the fort was progressing well when Nicolas and his father sailed down the Mobile River. It would be finished in a couple of months. Nicolas looked forward to the time when his father completed his work on the island so the family could move to La Mobile.

When they got to Massacre Island, Nicolas ran up the beach. He hugged his mother and François and slapped Simon playfully on the head. As they walked to their camp, Simon asked a million questions. Nicolas thought, he seems younger than when I left. He couldn't quite figure out the difference, but something had changed.

Nicolas was so anxious to get to the mound that he couldn't keep his mind on the conversation with his family. As soon as his father went to the warehouse, Nicolas said to his mother, "I've got to do something, but when I get back, I'll tell you and Simon everything I did." Without waiting for permission, he ran off in the direction of the warehouse. When he was out of sight, he turned and headed southwest.

He thought, I've wanted to know if there was a massacre or what happened to the people ever since I've been on this island. I'm going to run all the way to the mound, because I'm not changing my mind. He had to stop a couple of times to catch his breath, but he kept repeating, "I going to do it. I'm going to do it!" With André's directions in his head, he went straight to the place and ran right to the top of the mound without slowing down. "This isn't as high as I expected, and it certainly isn't a mountain!" he said out loud. He fell on his hands and knees and dug in the earth. He soon came across bones and a skull with traces of red on it. Sitting back on his heels, he looked toward the gulf. He thought

of all he'd heard from sailors who told of hurricanes that-blew gigantic waves across the islands. Nicolas imagined strong winds and waves tearing into the mound and scattering the bones. After a few minutes, he slowly pushed the bones back into the sandy soil and carefully covered them. Instead of feeling scared, he felt a deep sadness. Mothers and grandmothers had mourned for the people in this mound just like the two women he'd seen mourning for the little boy.

Nicolas looked up, and the winter sun warmed his face. He breathed in the salty air as he listened to the waves breaking on the shore.

LIFE
IN
LA LOUISIANE

1660–1700

In the late 1600s, when beaver hats became fashionable in Europe, there was a great demand for "brown gold," as furs were called. Native people eagerly traded them for European goods such as guns, mirrors, and beads. French and British fur-trading companies battled to control trade with the Indians in New France (Canada) and the Great Lakes region.

In 1682, Robert Cavelier de La Salle traveled the Mississippi River from present-day St. Louis, Missouri, to the Gulf of Mexico. He claimed a huge area for France, including all or part of what are now thirty-one states. It was named La Louisiane (French Louisiana) in honor of King Louis XIV.

The king wanted a colony on the northern Gulf so *coureurs de bois,* the daring French traders, could bring furs down the river from the Mississippi Valley to be shipped to France. A strong French colony would open up trade with Spanish colonial ports and also divide Spanish lands in Florida from those in the American Southwest. In addition, it would hinder English (British) movement westward from the Atlantic coast.

Cavelier de La Salle planned to establish a settlement near the mouth of the Mississippi River in1685. With a group of over 400 soldiers and settlers, he sailed west across the Gulf of Mexico. Due to errors in navigation, he missed the mouth of the river, and his group came ashore in present-day Texas. After three failed attempts to locate the river's mouth, La Salle tried to find another French settlement farther north to get help for his colonists. Two men, angry over the hardships caused by his mistakes, murdered him in 1687. Only fifteen people survived from the colony, eight of them children.

When a peace treaty in 1697 ended the war in Europe, King Louis XIV again thought of establishing a colony on the Gulf coast. He chose Pierre Le Moyne d'Iberville, a war hero, to found the colony.

Pierre, born in Montreal in 1661, was the third son of Charles Le Moyne, an early pioneer who became one of Canada's wealthiest men. Pierre, usually called Iberville, was the most famous son of New France. As a French naval officer, he won many battles against the British.

When Iberville sailed from France in 1698 on his first voyage to French Louisiana, his eighteen-year-old brother, Jean-Baptiste Le Moyne de Bienville, was with him. Other brothers followed on later voyages. The ships arrived on the northern Gulf coast in January of 1699. Iberville, Bienville, and several others explored an island at the mouth of Mobile Bay. Iberville named it Isle Massacre, because they found over sixty skulls and a pile of bones.

The ships continued sailing west. Some of the men stayed at present-day Ship Island on the coast of Mississippi, while Iberville, Bienville, and others explored parts of present-day Mississippi and Louisiana.

A group consisting mostly of French Canadians experienced in wilderness survival, and buccaneers (pirates) from Saint-Domingue (present-day Haiti) went with Iberville and Bienville some distance up the Mississippi River.

After descending the river, Iberville selected a site to build a fort at present-day Ocean Springs, Mississippi, on Biloxi Bay. In 1699 there were 81 on the roll of Fort Maurepas, including 75 men and six cabin boys, but no French women or children. Fort Maurepas, the official name of the fort, served as capital of La Louisiane (French Louisiana) from 1699–1702. It was often called Fort Biloxi.

In May of 1699, Iberville returned to France. He made a second voyage to La Louisiane in the fall and sailed back in May of 1700 in order to avoid hurricanes. He continued to seek a suitable location for the permanent colonial capital. Many men had died from diseases at Fort Maurepas, so he wanted a place with healthier conditions and more protection from storms.

1701–1702

French ships sailing to La Louisiane usually stopped at Saint-Domingue on the island of Hispaniola to take on fresh water, supplies, and livestock. On Iberville's third voyage, the *Palmier* had to be repaired there because lightning had struck the ship's mainmast. After leaving Saint-Domingue, Iberville became critically ill from an abscess in his side. The ship's doctor performed emergency surgery, but Iberville was still in serious condition when his ships arrived in Pensacola in mid-December. Two priests, who were surgeons from Veracruz, Mexico, were at the Presidio Santa María de Galve (present-day Pensacola, FL) and they gave him additional medical help. The Spanish *presidio* included Fort San Carlos de Austria and a small village with a church.

Spain and France were now at peace, and Iberville brought news that King Louis XIV's grandson had become king of Spain. Even though the Spanish didn't trust the French, and vice versa, they needed each other. In 1699, one of Iberville's ships rescued the Spanish commandant and his crew when their ship wrecked. Later, Bienville sent a boat to Santa María de Galve returning Spanish deserters who had come to Fort Maurepas seeking help. When Iberville's ships anchored in Pensacola Bay in 1701, he learned that a Spanish supply ship had not arrived. He gave the people there food and supplies from his ships. He also sent a sailboat with a crew of sixteen men to get provisions for them from the Spanish settlement in Veracruz, Mexico. In return for these favors, the Spanish allowed the *Renommée* to stay anchored in Pensacola Bay until Iberville sailed for France in April of 1702. They loaned Iberville four boats to transfer cargo from the *Renommée* to Massacre Island and on to La Mobile. This give-and-take relationship lasted through the colony's early years.

The Spanish officer in charge of Santa María de Galve had bad news for Iberville. Over sixty men, including the commandant, had died at Fort Maurepas in a three-month period. Bienville was now in command of the fort. With this information, Iberville decided to build a new fort immediately—Fort Louis de La Louisiane. He chose a place on the Mobile River now called Twenty-seven Mile Bluff. This river to the interior country could be used for exploration and trade. The site was just south of the Mobilian villages. Iberville hoped the Mobilians would help defend the French colony against raids by the Alabama tribe, who favored the English. He also wanted to get extra corn from the Mobilians. In addition, the location was close enough to Pensacola to encourage trade with the Spanish.

Bienville left only a major and a garrison of twenty men at Fort Maurepas when he sailed to Port Dauphin at Massacre Island with supplies.

Iberville was well enough by February of 1702 to travel to Massacre Island and then to Fort Louis and La Mobile to check on construction. He left Bienville in command of the colony when he sailed for France.

Jean-Baptiste Le Moyne de Bienville was a builder of colonies as well as an explorer. In 1699, at the age of nineteen, he went to the Mississippi River with Iberville to help establish Fort Boulaye in present-day Louisiana. He was commandant at Fort Boulaye, Fort Maurepas, and by the age of twenty-two, Fort Louis. He could communicate in many Indian languages, and he spent much time exploring the territory and making alliances with Native people. Bienville's personality helped keep peace among the Mobilians, Tomés, and other small Indian nations. They liked him very much, but they also feared him. He learned their ways and dressed like them when they went into battle together. When Alabama warriors killed three of Bienville's men in 1703, he called together the Mobilians, the Pascagoula, the Little Tomés and the Choctaw to avenge the men's blood.

War preparations at Mauvilla included dances by the warriors in the town plaza. The headmen and old men encouraged the youth, flogged until their blood ran, to bear their pain gracefully as the warriors would in the battle. Perhaps Bienville, caught up in the activities, either allowed his chest to be tattooed with figures of snakes or did it himself; the details are not known.

Various members of Nicolas (the father) de La Salle's family from Paris had served France in government jobs for years. He had two brothers who died while working in high commissary positions (in charge of supplies). He came to New France (Canada) as a young man of about sixteen and stayed for seven years. While in his twenties, he went with Cavelier de La Salle on the 1682 voyage to the mouth of the Mississippi River. He wrote an account of his experiences during the journey. After the group returned to New France, he and two others accompanied the explorer to France in 1683. Cavelier de La Salle reported the results of the historic trip to officials and got support for settling a colony up the Mississippi

River to guard the important waterway and set up trading operation. When he set sail for Louisiana in 1684 to found a colony, Nicolas de La Salle was a crew member on the ship. Apparently as part of the crew, he returned to France and did not stay with the colonists. The feelings he expresses in the story are my thoughts, but most likely he would not have continued to travel with the explorer if he had not respected him. Nicolas de La Salle was working for the Navy at the port of Toulon, France, when he learned of Iberville's expedition of 1701. His wife, Madelaine Chartroux, was from Toulon, and Nicolas, Simon, and François, were born there.

In January of 1702, Nicolas (the son) was 8 1/2 years old, Simon was 7, and François was about 4. I followed their father's example, however, and said they were older. Nicolas was large for his age at thirteen, so his father claimed he was sixteen, hoping that Commandant Bienville would give him a high-paying job. Nicolas was capable of bearing arms (serving as a soldier), spoke Native languages well, and was skilled in the way of the wilderness, according to his father.

Information about Nicolas and Simon comes from what their father and others said about them. Even though their words and actions are fictitious, many of their experiences are based on documented events. The scene of Nicolas saving Simon is based on weather conditions of January 5, 1702, and a description of a similar situation described by Father Paul Du Ru. The soldiers, Canadians, and even the La Salle family lived in makeshift lean-tos on Massacre Island, at least when they first arrived. And even modern campers along the Gulf coast have had experiences similar to Nicolas's with the cockroach (Palmetto bug). The "roach dance"—shedding clothes at lightning speed while wildly jumping and twisting—is hilarious to onlookers but not at all funny to the victim.

Information about the period of history from 1698 to 1721 often comes from the accounts of André-Joseph Pénigault. Born in La Rochelle, France, on December 30, 1677, André was the son of a butcher who couldn't read. His godfather, though, André L'Ortie, was a well-known Protestant minister and the author of many books. He might have inspired André to write about his life and adventures. André writes that since the age of fifteen, he had an urge to see foreign lands. In 1698, at the age of eighteen, he sailed with Iberville as an indentured servant of Pierre-Charles Le Sueur. André was an adventurous young ship's carpenter skilled in building and repairing boats. Since he also served as an interpreter, he was often chosen to go on exciting expeditions. He claims that he wrote of his experiences year-by-year while in La Louisiane, but part of it might have been written years later. (Perhaps for this reason, some of the dates are not correct, but his writings are entertaining and informative.) He wrote about Native people—their lives and social customs—in a way that did not judge them. The French were shown in a fair and honest manner, neither as heroes nor villains. Even though André was two years older than Bienville, he writes about the commandant with respect. André witnessed the flogging of the Mobilian children as described in the story by Monsieur La Salle. Since André saw the pile of skulls and bones, Nicolas's conclusion about the massacre is based on what André wrote. The English edition of André's book is *Fleur de Lys and Calumet: Being the Pénicaut Narrative of French Adventure in Louisiana.*

Many teenage cabin boys, such as the character of Claude, lived with Native people in order to build friendships and learn their languages. This was extremely important during the first years of a French settlement. (The practice followed the example of Cavelier de La Salle. Captain John Smith also had cabin boys live with Indians near Jamestown.) Six boys came on Iberville's 1699 expedition and went to four tribes to learn their dialects. Twelve more boys came in 1702 to become interpreters.

The idea of the alligator attacking Claude's dog came from André's account in 1700 of an incident in present-day Louisiana. He writes, "It was called *Rivière-aux-Chiens* [Dog River] because a crocodile [actually an alligator] ate up one of our dogs there." Dog River that flows into Mobile Bay might have gotten its name in the same way. In March of 1702, Iberville wrote in his journal, "We are naming it *Rivière-aux-Chiens.*"

The actions of Nicolas, Simon, and Red Bird are

from descriptions of first encounters with Native people. The scene with "lots of spirit" and "lost spirit" expresses the ideas of some Indians on bravery. Nicolas might have visited a Mobilian village, and an Indian boy did live with the French to learn their language. In 1700 the headman of the Pascagoula tribe went with Bienville and two Frenchmen to visit the *mingo* of the Mobilians. They took him a present and invited him to Fort Maurepas to make an alliance. The Mobilians wanted the French nearby to protect them from tribes encouraged by the English (British) to raid villages and enslave their people. They also wanted guns. In return, the Mobilian nation allowed La Mobile to be built on their tribal lands. By providing corn, venison, and other foods, they kept the settlers from starving. They also protected the colonists from hostile tribes.

With limited information available on the Mobilian nation, many details in the story, including the language, are based on their ancestors, the Choctaw. The "Mobilian Jargon" was used for trade over a large part of what is now the United States. It was easily learned by Europeans and Indians because of limited words and simple grammar. When the Mobilians talked with each other, they used the Mobilian language.

Frenchmen and others documented Choctaw burial customs. However, customs, traditions, and styles changed over time and varied from place to place—just as they do today. The one record of Mobilian burial customs, written about 25 years after the French settled the area, is different in some ways from the burial described in the story.

Religion was important in the lives of eighteenth-century people. Priests and missionaries were vital to troops and colonists, since death was always close at hand. Most of the colonists of La Louisiane were Roman Catholic. Father Paul Du Ru, a Jesuit priest, was chaplain on Iberville's second voyage in 1699. Chaplains recited daily prayers, held Mass, heard confessions, and prayed for the dying. They went on expeditions and prayed for the soldiers before battles. When the colonists arrived at La Mobile, the priests performed weddings and baptized babies.

Father Du Ru's journal provides information about priests, and I've used it to describe Father Dongé's activities. Father Du Ru built an altar from canes, and his servant made a large cross at Fort Boulaye. I have assumed that these were also made at Massacre Island. In André's journal, he tells of a place on the Mississippi River where Iberville marked a spot with a cross. Getting down on their knees, the men sang a song, which greatly surprised the Indians. The Frenchmen let the Natives know that the cross was something greatly valued in their religion and should not be destroyed. After Father Du Ru sailed for France with Iberville in April of 1702, Father Dongé became chaplain. Father Dongé, who had arrived that year, was described as a cheerful and compassionate priest.

Pirates flocked to Hispaniola, Jamaica, and deserted

islands around the Caribbean Sea from 1500–1800. Their targets at first were ships carrying cargoes of gold, silver, and precious gems. However, by the late 1600s, they were attacking any ship they suspected of having valuable cargo in the Caribbean and the Gulf of Mexico. They also raided settlements along the coasts.

Pirates called themselves different names—freebooters, buccaneers, and corsairs—but they were still pirates. "Freebooter" came from a Dutch word meaning "free booty." The valuables from the raid were split among the pirates. There were "freebooters" at Fort Maurepas and Old Mobile. "Buccaneer" came from the French word *boucan,* a wooden grill for smoking meat. The original buccaneers hunted wild cattle and hogs on the western end of Hispaniola (Saint-Domingue and now Haiti) and dried the meat. Ships' captains eagerly bought the dried meat, because it didn't spoil on long voyages. A "privateer" was a ship, or ship's captain, carrying official papers that permitted the captain to attack enemy (but not neutral) ships in time of war. French corsairs or "racers" used small vessels to attack far larger ships. The French government often used corsairs as privateers against the Spanish.

In 1701, Iberville's ships were chased by a fleet of pirates during a storm as described by Nicolas.

The Veracruz raid that Nicolas described to Simon in the story has been called the cruelest and most daring up to that time in the Gulf of Mexico. Laurens de Graff was one of the pirate leaders. Possibly of Spanish ancestry, he had special knowledge of the Spanish possessions when he sailed under English or French flags. The Spanish called him "Lorencillo." He was their most feared and hated pirate, so they were quite surprised to see him in Pensacola as Iberville's pilot and interpreter. Laurens de Graff sailed with Iberville from France in October of 1698. He had either become a worthwhile citizen or Iberville had lowered the standards for his crew in order to gain information from the pirate and his buccaneers. (French pirates of western Hispaniola were the most knowledgeable pilots of the northern Gulf coast.) Perhaps Iberville wanted to avoid Cavelier de La Salle's mistake. La Salle had refused pirates' help, because he hadn't had the King's permission. And his errors in navigation cost the lives of a great number of people.

AFTER THE STORY

Bienville had a difficult task leading colonists who faced unbelievable hardships. Many he supervised were older than he and probably thought him unwise because of his age. Some colonists born in France also considered themselves socially higher than the Canadian-born commandant. One of Bienville's strongest traits was single-mindedness—he persevered when others gave up. Long after others thought it wise to change the location of La Mobile, he refused. However, serious flooding finally forced him to agree to the move in the summer of 1711. The new site was near the mouth of the Mobile River, close to the place where Charles Levasseur planted a cross in 1700. After the move, the first site was referred to as Old Mobile. Antoine Cadillac became governor of French Louisiana in 1712, but Bienville stayed in Mobile and served as his assistant for three years. In 1718, Bienville founded the city of New Orleans. He spent over thirty years in French Louisiana. In 1767 at the age of 87, he died in France.

Before Iberville left La Mobile, he felt it was necessary to have "the straightest path possible," between La Mobile and Pensacola "to be able to come and go as quickly as possible in times of need." So an overland trail was built through the wilderness from Santa María de Galve to a bay on the Spanish River (Tensaw River). When it was completed, Bienville persuaded Canadian Philippe Minette to settle near the mouth of the river. Philippe had come to Fort Maurepas on Iberville's voyage in 1699. When the lots had been assigned in La Mobile, Philippe had received one of the smallest. Since he was willing to relocate, which no doubt meant more land, he ended up having a bay and a town (Bay Minette, AL) named for him.

Iberville had planned to return to La Mobile in 1703, but war in Europe delayed him. He died in Havana from yellow fever in 1706 without ever returning.

Port Dauphin had few people living there after everyone had left for La Mobile—there were usually only a few guards at the warehouse. Finally several families moved to the island. Some carried on private trade with passing ships. Unfortunately in 1710, a ship with a Jamaican pirate crew raided the island. The keeper of the warehouse and a low-ranking naval officer, the only two officials on the island at the time, were taken to the pirate ship and held as hostages. Over thirty pirates came ashore in rowboats and took the island without a shot being fired. The inhabitants—too disorganized to resist—were herded into several houses. The pirates spent two days loading everything of value onto their ship. Before leaving on the third day, they tortured people they thought were hiding cash. Then they set fire to the warehouse and all the buildings except the houses holding captives and a few houses far away. A Canadian *voyageur* landed his small boat at a distant house as the pirates were leaving. He didn't know the cause of the fire, but spotting a looter near the warehouse, he shot and killed him. When the looter didn't return to the ship, the pirates thought a rescue party had arrived. The next day, the pirate captain sent a small group to see how well the island was now defended. Four villagers and the Canadian spread out and fired shots at them, slipping around and firing from different directions. It appeared there was a large group, so the pirates returned to the ship and soon sailed away. The attack proved that Massacre Island needed a strong defense. A wooden fort was soon built to protect the settlement from attacks.

Bienville had said that several persons "consider the name of Massacre as harsh." So, in 1711, Massacre Island became Isle Dauphine (now Dauphin Island), and the port was named Port Dauphin. As many as 20 homes were built along Port Dauphin's one street by 1717, but a terrible hurricane that year blocked the port. After that, the number of people on the island began to decrease.

The shell mounds on Massacre Island date from the Mississippian Period (AD 1100–1550). For centuries, Indians had visited the island, most likely in winter and spring, to gather oysters and fish. Over the years, huge mounds of oyster shells accumulated. The burial mound on Massacre Island was probably either a low sand mound (about 4' high and 20–40' across) like others in the area, or a shell midden (trash pit) that was used for burial. Archaeologists tend to agree with André Pénigault's explanation of the skeletons on Massacre Island, instead of the theory that the people were victims of war. Pénigault was in a position to know which Native tribe used the island for burials, even though he seems to have exaggerated the number of skeletons. In his account, he writes: "We became terrified upon finding such a prodigious [large] number of human skeletons that they formed a mountain, there were so many of them. We learned afterwards that this was a numerous nation who, being pursued and having withdrawn to this region, had almost all died here of sickness; and as the manner of savages is to gather together all the bones of the dead, they had carried them into this spot. This nation was called Mobila, and a small number of them survive."

The number of Mobilians continued to decrease as well as those of other Native American tribes. Diseases brought by the Europeans "mowed down whole tribes, since the arrival of the French in these parts," writes Father Le Maire in 1714. The five Mobilian villages of 1700 evidently was down to only one by the mid-1720s, due to disease and enemy raids. Over the centuries to follow, Indians suffered greatly and sacrificed much to have given so freely in the beginning to their French neighbors. Native Americans still live in the area of Old Mobile. Perhaps they are the descendants of the Mobilians and others tribes that lived along the river.

The last recorded information that I've found on Nicolas and Simon indicates that they were soldiers during their teens.

Fort Louis de La Louisiane was renamed Fort Condé in 1720 in honor of a prominent French family. From 1724–35 the French built a permanent brick and mortar fort within the temporary stockade.

We, along the Gulf coast, owe a debt of gratitude to our Canadian neighbors to the North. Iberville, Beinville, many of their relatives, the *voyageurs,* and Canadian colonists gained the foothold for France along the Gulf of Mexico. However, without the support of the French government, this would not have been possible. Individuals from France, families such as the Nicolas La Salle family, and—beginning in 1704—the Cassette Girls brought their culture from France as French Canadians brought their variations of the French culture.

In Mobile, Alabama, there are many reminders of the French: azaleas and Mardi Gras in the springtime, French style homes, street names, Fort Condé, and Bienville Square. Few know of Massacre Island, but more tourists discover the beautiful water and white beaches of Dauphin Island each year. I am grateful to the men and women, boys and girls, who survived incredible hardships to leave a French heritage on the Gulf coast.

Anne Chancey Dalton

GLOSSARY OF FRENCH WORDS

Au contraire!	(oh kon-TRAIR)	On the contrary!
au revoir	(oh reh-VWAR)	good-bye
bébé	(bay-BAY)	baby
bien	(byen)	good
Bien sûr!	(byen syur)	But of course!
bon	(bohn)	good
bonjour	(bohn-ZHOOR)	hello
Cap-français	(CAP-franh-SAY)	(In present-day Haiti)
capote	(kah-POAT)	coat with hood
chienne	(shyen)	female dog
chocolat	(sho-ko-LAH)	chocolate
coureurs de bois	(coy-UR duh bwa)	French traders
Dauphine	(DOE feen)	(Name of a boat)
Fort Maurepas	(MOR-eh-pah)	(In Ocean Springs, MS)
madame	(mah-DAHM)	Mrs. or madam
Mais oui!	(may wee)	But, yes!
merci	(mehr-SEE)	thank you
Mon Dieu!	(mohn dyuh)	My God! or Good heavens!
mon fils	(mohn fees)	my son
monsieur	(muh-SYER)	Mister or sir
non	(nohn)	no
oui	(wee)	yes
oui madame	(wee mah-DAHM)	yes, ma'am
oui monsieur	(wee muh-SYER)	yes, sir
Palmier	(PAL-me-ay)	(name of a ship)
pardon	(pahr-DOHN)	excuse me
par excellence	(pahr ek-seh-LAHNS)	excellent
Renommée	(RU-num-ay)	(name of a ship)
Riviére aux Chiens	(RIV-ee-air oh shyen)	Dog River
toque	(tow-KUH)	cap
un, deux, trois	(un), (duh), (twah)	one, two, three
voyageur	(vwoy-YAH-zhur)	one who takes goods along the fur-trade route

GLOSSARY OF CHOCTAW WORDS

Chishno pisah yukpah siah it tikana su.
    (shish-no pee-sah yuk-puh see-ah it tikana soo)
                    I am glad to see you my friend.

Falamochi!	(fa-la-MOO-chee)	Throw it back!
Hokli!	(HOK-li)	Catch!
Hushi Humma	(HOO-shi HOO-ma)	Bird Red or Red Bird
ishtaboli	(ISH-ta-bol-lee)	ball-play or stickball
itta bena	(IT-tah BEE-nah)	home in the woods
mingo* (minco)	(MIN-go)	headman, village or tribe chief
Na foni aiowa	(na-fowni-a-o-wa)	bone-pickers or bone-gatherers
oski kauwa	(AW-ski KA-wa)	bundles of split cane used to measure time

*John R. Swanton in *Source Material for the Social and Ceremonial Life of the Choctaw Indians* uses information from an early Frech memoir that translates it "mingo," and that is the current Choctaw pronunciation.

Select Bibliography

Approximately fifty books and periodicals were used in research for this book. The following is a select list of those used most often.

Ariès, Philippe. *Centuries of Childhood: A Social History of Family Life*. Translated from French by Robert Baldick.NewYork: Alfred A. Knopf, 1962.

Brohaugh, William. *English Through the Ages. Cincinnati: Writer's Digest Books, 1998*.

Butler, Ruth Lapham. Translated with introduction and notes from a manuscript in the Newberry Library. *Journal of Paul du Ru: Missionary Priest to Louisiana*. Chicago: The Caxton Club, 1934. Reprinted in Fairfield, WA: Ye Galleon Press, 1997.

Brown, Virginia Pounds and Laurella Owens. *The World of the Southern Indians*. Leeds, AL: Beechwood Books, 1983.

Chartrand, René. *Canadian Military History, Vol 1:1000–1754*. Montreal: Art Global, 1993.

Deplanne, Véronique. *Legacies of a French Empire in North America*. Virginia Beach: The Donning Co./Publishers, 1999.

Doherty, Kieran. *Soldiers, Cavaliers, and Planters: Soldiers of the Southeastern Colonies*. Minneapolis: The Oliver Press, Inc., 1999.

Du Pratz, M. Le Page. *The History of Louisiana*. English trans. By Henry C. Dethloff. Baton Rouge: Claitor's Pub. Division, 1972.

Giraud, Marcel. *A History of French Louisiana*. Trans. by Joseph C. Lambert. Vol. 1. Baton Rouge: Louisiana State U. Press, 1974.

Higginbotham, Jay. *Fort Maurepas: The Birth of Louisiana*. Mobile: Colonial Books, 1968.

-----. *The Mobile Indians.* Mobile: Sir Key's Printing Co., 1966.

-----. *Old Mobile: Fort Louis de la Louisiane, 1702–1711.* Tuscaloosa:
The University of Alabama Press, 1977.

----- and Francis Escoffier. Translated and edited. *A Voyage to
Dauphin Island in 1720.* Mobile: Museum of the City of Mobile,
1974.

Johnson, Mary Moyars, Judy Forbes, and Kathy Delaney. *Historic
Colonial French Dress.* Grand Rapids: Smoke & Fire News, 1977.

Kennedy, Jo Myrle. *Dauphin Island, Alabama: French Possession,
1699–1763.* Selma, AL: Coffee Printing Company, 1976.

La Harpe, Jean-Baptiste Benard. Translated and edited by Joan Cain
and Virginia Koenig. Edited and annotated by Glenn
R. Conrad. *The Historical Journal of the Establishment of the French in
Louisiana.* Lafayette: Center for Louisiana Studies, University of
Southwestern Louisiana, 1971.

McWilliams, Richebourg Gaillard. *Fleur de Lys and Calumet.* Baton
Rouge: Louisiana State University Press, 1953.

-----. Translated and edited. *Iberville's Gulf Journals.* Tuscaloosa:
The University of Alabama Press, 1981.

Mitchell, Patricia B. *French Cooking in Early America.* Chatham, VA:
Patricia Mitchell, 1991.

Parkman, Francis. *La Salle and the Discovery of the Great West.*
Jon Krakauer, Series Ed., New York: The Modern Library, 1999.

Pirates of the Spanish Main. By the editors of *American Heritage:
The Magazine of History.* New York: American Heritage Publishing
Co., Inc., 1961.

Santa María de Galve: A Story of Survival. Edited by Virginia Parks.
Pensacola Historical Society, 1998.

Swanton, John R. *Source Material for the Social and Ceremonial Life of the Choctaw Indians.* Birmingham: Birmingham Public Lib. Press, 1993.

Waselkov, Gregory A. *Old Mobile Archaeology.* Mobile: Center for Archaeological Studies, University of South Alabama, 1999.

-----. "*Old Mobile Project Newsletter,*" Vol. 15, Fall 1997.

-----. "*Old Mobile Project Newsletter,*" Vol. 16, Spring 1998.

-----. "*Old Mobile Project Newsletter,*" Vol. 17, Fall 1998.

----- and Bonnie L. Gums with contributions by Kristen J. Gremillion & Diane E. Silvia. *Plantation Archaeology at Rivière aux Chiens, ca. 1725-1848.* June, 2000.

Weddle, Robert S. The French Thorn: *Rival Explorers in the Spanish Sea, 1682–1762.* College Station: Texas A&M University Press, 1991.

-----. *Wilderness Manhunt: The Spanish Search for La Salle.* College Station: Texas A&M University Press, 1999.

Anne Chancey Dalton likes mystery and adventure. And since historical research is similar to solving mysteries, she has traveled from Canada to cemeteries in Texas to find clues. She has participated in archaeological digs in Virginia and at Old Mobile and Fort Morgan in Alabama. Anne has performed in dinner theaters in Florida, clowning in Costa Rica, and historical interpretations around the USA and in England. She enjoys white-water rafting through the tropical rain forests of Costa Rica.

A freelance writer for twenty-five years, Mrs. Dalton's work includes stories for reading textbooks, church school curricula, and magazine articles.

Anne and her husband, Perry, live in Mobile, Alabama and Panama City, Florida. They have 10 children and 30-something grandchildren.

Dave C. Edwards, a native of Middletown, Ohio, is a freelance artist. He received his Bachelor of Fine Arts Degree from Miami University in Oxford, Ohio, and has lived on the Gulf Coast for over twenty years.

Dave's work reflects his love of nature and history, which he preserves in a visual art form. He uses a variety of mediums such as oils, acrylics, pen and ink, and watercolors to uniquely portray realistic scenes. His illustrations have appeared in national educational and historical magazines. Having studied and researched the history of the Gulf Coast for years, Dave is also involved in colonial-period living history programs in the southern coastal states.

The artist resides in Pensacola, Florida, with his wife and daughter.